Duke Ellington

These and other titles are included in The Importance
Of biography series:

Alexander the Great	Adolf Hitler
Muhammad Ali	Harry Houdini
Louis Armstrong	Thomas Jefferson
Clara Barton	Chief Joseph
Napoleon Bonaparte	Malcolm X
Rachel Carson	Margaret Mead
Charlie Chaplin	Michelangelo
Cesar Chavez	Wolfgang Amadeus Mozart
Winston Churchill	Sir Isaac Newton
Cleopatra	Richard M. Nixon
Christopher Columbus	Georgia O'Keeffe
Hernando Cortes	Louis Pasteur
Marie Curie	Pablo Picasso
Amelia Earhart	Jackie Robinson
Thomas Edison	Anwar Sadat
Albert Einstein	Margaret Sanger
Duke Ellington	Oskar Schindler
Dian Fossey	John Steinbeck
Benjamin Franklin	Jim Thorpe
Galileo Galilei	Mark Twain
Martha Graham	Pancho Villa
Stephen Hawking	H. G. Wells
Jim Henson	

Duke Ellington

by
Adam Woog

Lucent Books, P.O. Box 289011, San Diego, CA 92198-9011

Library of Congress Cataloging-in-Publication Data

Woog, Adam, 1953-
    Duke Ellington / by Adam Woog.
        p. cm.—(The importance of)
    Includes bibliographical references and index.
    ISBN 1-56006-073-5 (alk. pap.)
    1. Ellington, Duke, 1899-1974—Juvenile literature.   2. Jazz
musicians—United States—Biography—Juvenile literature.
I. Title.   II. Series.
ML3930.E44W66   1996
781.65'092—dc20   95-5008
[B]   CIP
                                                                          AC MN

Copyright 1996 by Lucent Books, Inc., P.O. Box 289011,
San Diego, California 92198-9011

Printed in the U.S.A.

Contents

Foreword

THE IMPORTANCE OF biography series deals with individuals who have made a unique contribution to history. The editors of the series have deliberately chosen to cast a wide net and include people from all fields of endeavor. Individuals from politics, music, art, literature, philosophy, science, sports, and religion are all represented. In addition, the editors did not restrict the series to individuals whose accomplishments have helped change the course of history. Of necessity, this criterion would have eliminated many whose contribution was great, though limited. Charles Darwin, for example, was responsible for radically altering the scientific view of the natural history of the world. His achievements continue to impact the study of science today. Others, such as Chief Joseph of the Nez Percé, played a pivotal role in the history of their own people. While Joseph's influence does not extend much beyond the Nez Percé, his nonviolent resistance to white expansion and his continuing role in protecting his tribe and his homeland remain an inspiration to all.

These biographies are more than factual chronicles. Each volume attempts to emphasize an individual's contributions both in his or her own time and for posterity. For example, the voyages of Christopher Columbus opened the way to European colonization of the New World. Unquestionably, his encounter with the New World brought monumental changes to both Europe and the Americas in his day. Today, however, the broader impact of Columbus's voyages is being critically scrutinized. *Christopher Columbus,* as well as every biography in The Importance Of series, includes and evaluates the most recent scholarship available on each subject.

Each author includes a wide variety of primary and secondary source quotations to document and substantiate his or her work. All quotes are footnoted to show readers exactly how and where biographers derive their information, as well as provide stepping stones to further research. These quotations enliven the text by giving readers eyewitness views of the life and times of each individual covered in The Importance Of series.

Finally, each volume is enhanced by photographs, bibliographies, chronologies, and comprehensive indexes. For both the casual reader and the student engaged in research, The Importance Of biographies will be a fascinating adventure into the lives of people who have helped shape humanity's past and present, and who will continue to shape its future.

IMPORTANT DATES IN THE LIFE OF DUKE ELLINGTON

1899
Edward Kennedy Ellington is born in Washington, D.C., on April 29.

1913
Composes first song.

1918
Marries Edna Thompson.

1919
Son, Mercer, is born.

1923
Plays with Wilbur Sweatman's band in Harlem; returns to New York City later that year when the Washingtonians gets its first major engagements.

1924
Formally becomes the Washingtonians' leader; band makes first recording.

1926
Begins recording series for Vocalion; writes first theme song, "East Saint Louis Toodle-Oo."

1927
Band name changes to Duke Ellington and His Famous Orchestra; band opens at the Cotton Club and broadcasts nationally on CBS Radio.

1929
Separates from Edna; band appears in first film, *Black and Tan Fantasy*.

1930
Brings family to New York; band backs Gershwin show, and appears in first Hollywood film.

1932
Band is chosen by *Pittsburgh Courier* as the top band in the country; Ellington plays and lectures at Columbia University; *Creole Rhapsody* wins New York Schools of Music Award for best new work by an American composer.

1933
Band makes first trip to Europe.

1940
Classic all-star band is assembled, including Billy Strayhorn, Jimmy Blanton, Ray Nance, and Ben Webster; band grosses $1 million for the first time.

1941
Jump for Joy premieres in Los Angeles.

1943
Black, Brown, and Beige premieres at Carnegie Hall.

1956
Makes a triumphant comeback appearance at the Newport Jazz Festival.

1958
Is presented to Queen Elizabeth II.

1959
Writes film score for *Anatomy of a Murder*.

1960s
Begins making extensive overseas tours.

1963
Is diagnosed with lung cancer.

1965
Performs First Sacred Concert at Grace Cathedral, San Francisco.

1968
Performs Second Sacred Concert at Cathedral of Saint John the Divine, New York City.

1969
Seventieth birthday party at the White House.

1973
Performs Third Sacred Concert at Westminster Abbey, London.

1974
Dies on May 24 of pneumonia brought on by lung cancer.

"We Love You Madly"

Duke Ellington, whose contours have something of the swell and sweep of a large, erect bear and whose color is that of coffee with a strong dash of cream, has been described by European music critics as one of the world's immortals.

—Richard O. Boyer, *The New Yorker*

No other American composer has been more honored than Duke Ellington. Recognizing his contributions to music and culture, France and Ethiopia presented him with their highest awards. Four other nations issued postage stamps with his picture. The Swedish Academy of Music made him the only nonclassical member in its two-hundred-year history. And the United States gave him its highest civilian honor, the Presidential Medal of Freedom, at a birthday party for him at the White House.

All this reflects one single fact: Edward Kennedy Ellington changed the course of music forever.

Ellington was not merely a great composer. He was also a synthesizer; that is, he blended popular and Afro-American

Duke Ellington's unique flair and musical style earned him a place as one of history's most beloved bandleaders and composers.

musical styles with European classical music. Though he is associated with jazz, Ellington disliked the term and insisted it did not apply to him. As early as the 1930s, long before organized civil rights or the concept of "black is beautiful," Ellington proudly called his work "Negro music" or "the music of my people." He was, above all, an *American* composer. Critic Albert Murray, quoted in *Beyond Category*, noted, "I don't think anybody has achieved a higher synthesis of the American experience than Duke Ellington expressed in his music."[1] Perhaps the best term for his unique work is simply "Ellington music."

Ellington did much more than compose. He could not bear to write music that would rarely, if ever, be played, so he created the longest continuously operating big band in history to make real the sounds that flowed from his imagination. Even when it no longer was profitable, Ellington kept his band alive; he needed to hear daily what he had written the

Quintessentially American

Ellington tried always to blend into his music his experiences as both an American and a black man, as John Edward Hasse points out in this excerpt from his biography, Beyond Category.

"Though Ellington's music was deeply rooted in the African-American life he experienced in his native Washington, D.C., and in Harlem, his art is quintessentially [typically] American in its integration of the primary colors—European, African, and American—that form the rainbow culture of the United States. He often composed on American themes that affirmed the dual cultural identity of being simultaneously an American and an Afro-American, celebrated such American cultural heroes as Bert Williams, Louis Armstrong, and Martin Luther King, Jr., and affirmed his own and his people's struggle for complete citizenship.

Ellington's sound grew out of his experiences and those of his multihued company of players in urban, twentieth-century America. . . . Yet beyond being American, Ellington's music is joyously and positively human. What could be more affirming than to celebrate individuality; to unite differing musical personalities into a synergistic [interactive] ensemble, to communicate a range of human emotions from anger and sorrow to awe, humor, hope, love, and joy; and to express timeless values such as dignity, reverence, and freedom?"

Incredibly energetic and dedicated to his music, Ellington maintained the longest continuously performing big band in history.

night before. The result—thousands of recordings, dozens of orchestral pieces, scores of hit songs—continues to astonish and delight audiences worldwide.

With his band of eccentric geniuses in tow, he restlessly circled the globe, playing in everything from low dives to fine concert halls—an estimated twenty thousand appearances in a fifty-year career. At each concert Ellington told the audience, "We love you madly." Only when seriously ill at the very end did Ellington slow down, and even then he kept working from a hospital bed.

Ellington was a genius, but he was also a complex human. He was a black American who never lost his dignity or pride even as he overcame difficult obstacles to become a wealthy, beloved celebrity. He

was a tall, handsome charmer with a sly smile and amused eyes. He had limitless energy and was legendary for his love of food and women. But he was also famously disorganized, with methods of composing as eccentric as his lifestyle. And he was superstitious, shrewd, alternately sentimental and ruthless, self-centered, and manipulative. Through it all he remained utterly devoted to his music.

Duke Ellington was born one year before the beginning of the twentieth century, and he died seventy-five years later. He witnessed the rise of television, the Jazz Age, the Great Depression, two world wars, and the civil rights movement. In many ways his life parallels the best and worst of twentieth-century American life.

1 The Early Years

Many musicians acquire great technique, but taste is the final thing. I think taste is something you're born with. . . . Even a great hack has to have good taste, because he has to know what to steal.

—Duke Ellington

Washington, D.C., was an unusual place for Afro-Americans at the turn of the century. The states bordering it had outlawed slavery only a few decades before. Washington itself never had slaves, but it had been an important center for the slave trade, and the city was southern in its outlook. Blacks and whites were strictly separated; as late as 1922, when the Lincoln Memorial was dedicated, blacks sat in a separate, roped-off area.

The black community itself was sharply divided. At the top were descendants of people who had never been

Turn-of-the-century Washington, D.C., was home to the country's largest Afro-American population. The city's many black professionals and leaders served as positive role models, inspiring young blacks like Ellington to succeed.

slaves. Below them was a middle class of businesspeople, government workers, and professionals such as doctors and lawyers. Below them was a lower class, most of whom lived in poverty. There was little intermingling between these groups. Ellington recalled, "I don't know how many castes [social divisions] of Negroes there were in the city at that time, but I do know that if you decided to mix carelessly with another you would be told that one just did not do that sort of thing."[2]

On the other hand, Washington was a place of promise for many. Its population of eighty-seven thousand Afro-Americans was the largest of any U.S. city. It was home to such institutions as Howard University, one of the first colleges for Afro-Americans. And Washington's black leaders were models of education, ambition, and discipline. As author Mark Tucker put it, "Ellington may have spent his earliest years in a city deeply divided by race and class. But this same city inspired its black citizens to aim high and, in so doing, to move beyond category."[3]

Ellington's father, James Edward (right), worked as a butler for the family of a prominent doctor. From his easygoing father, Edward learned self-confidence and an appreciation of the finer things in life.

Birth of the Duke

Edward Kennedy Ellington was born in Washington on April 29, 1899, the first child of James Edward Ellington and Daisy Kennedy Ellington. He was delivered by a midwife at 2129 Ward Place NW, the home of his father's parents.

His mother, Daisy, the daughter of a police captain, was a soft-spoken beauty who had been raised from birth in the upper levels of black society. She was a high school graduate, quite an achievement then for a black woman. Daisy was rigidly

moral and quite prim; for instance, she refused to wear lipstick or makeup. She carried herself with dignity, dressed elegantly, and spoke properly at all times. As was usual for a woman in her position, she stayed at home to devote herself to her son.

J. E., as Ellington's father was known, was more easygoing and came from a humbler background. Though he was raised on a farm in North Carolina and had only a seventh-grade education, his outgoing nature and good manners had landed him a job as a butler for a prominent physician. He also moonlighted as caterer, including an occasional job at the White House. J. E. knew about all the finer things in life, whether it was wine, food, china, clothes, or cars. He was a good dancer, and he appreciated beautiful women. J. E. worked hard to care for his family. As Ellington wrote about his father in his memoirs, "He raised his family as though he were a millionaire. The best had to be carefully examined to make sure it was good enough for my mother."[4]

Raised in the Palm of the Hand

Daisy and J. E. coddled young Edward from the beginning. Over and over they told him that he was special, blessed. The boy could do no wrong, and nothing was denied him. When Edward was sick, Daisy sent for two doctors. When he started school, Daisy followed him to ensure his safety. Edward was better than other children, not subject to ordinary rules and so was rarely punished. As Ellington himself put it, speaking in the third person, "They raised him in the palm of the hand and gave him everything they thought he wanted. Finally, when he was about seven or eight, they let his feet touch the ground."[5]

From his father, Ellington learned manners, an appreciation of finery and women, a friendly bearing, and self-confidence. From his mother, he absorbed a hatred of conflict, a strong religious faith, and the unshakable belief that he was blessed. These traits stayed with Ellington all his life and earned him his famous nickname, Duke. As biographer James Lincoln Collier has noted:

> Anyone who knew Duke Ellington as an adult could see the results of this teaching in his every move: the good manners and proper speech carried to an extreme; his unyielding insistence that he be respected; the racial pride . . . and his need always to mingle with the "best" people.[6]

"They Loved Their Little Boy Very Much"

The first sentences in Ellington's memoirs, Music Is My Mistress, *indicate the book's sunny outlook and the positive spin that Ellington tried to put on everything in his life.*

"Once upon a time, a beautiful young lady and a very handsome young man fell in love and got married. They were a wonderful, compatible couple, and God blessed their marriage with a fine baby boy (eight pounds eight ounces). They loved their little boy very much. They raised him in the palm of the hand and gave him everything they thought he wanted. Finally, when he was about seven or eight, they let his feet touch the ground."

Ellington's only sibling, Ruth, was born when he was nineteen. As his parents' only child for so many years, Edward was showered with love and attention.

Edward was an only child until he was nineteen, when his sister Ruth was born. Only children are often, as Ellington himself said, "pampered and pampered, and spoiled rotten." But there may be another explanation for Daisy's lavish attention on him. She once had another child, who died tragically young. Details are not clear, but Ellington's birth certificate lists him as the family's second child. This loss no doubt made Daisy doubly anxious to ensure her boy's safety.

Young Edward's devotion to Daisy was just as complete. She was, he often said later, the only person he wanted to please.

When Daisy died in 1935, he was devastated. Ellington's sister, Ruth, once remarked, "He said that when he was a little boy and sitting on his mother's lap, he looked into her face and he knew that she was the most beautiful mother in the world. And he felt that way about her until the day she died."[7]

Life was comfortable for young Edward. He always had good food and a fine home. Summers were spent at the seashore. Their neighborhood in Northwest Washington was prosperous and full of children. Both Daisy and J. E. had relatives in the area, so Edward had no shortage of aunts, uncles, and cousins to pamper or play with him. In his memoirs Ellington recalls visiting the houses of aunts and uncles every Sunday with his cousin to see who had the best food.

"Three Educations"

Several other factors figured in Ellington's early development. In school he showed a flair for visual art. He entered high school in 1913 and could have gone to M Street, the nation's first public high school for Afro-Americans and the best of Washington's black high schools. Instead he chose Armstrong Manual Training School to study commercial art. The choice seems a little strange for Ellington, who even as an adolescent was conscious of prestige, for Armstrong was a rough place. Perhaps young Edward felt that a practical skill would serve him best. Even at Armstrong, however, he received lessons in behavior. He recalled that his teacher would explain that "when we went out into the world, we would have the grave responsibility of being practically always on stage. . . . As representatives of the Negro race we were to command respect for our people."[8]

Edward also received more informal forms of education. Like most middle-class homes of the era, the Ellington house had a piano, and both Daisy and J. E. sang and played light operatic arias, sentimental songs, and religious pieces. At age seven or eight Edward took piano lessons from a teacher named Marietta Clinkscales. (Later in life Ellington had to repeatedly convince interviewers that Mrs. Clinkscales was not a made-up name.) But the lessons did not stick, and Ellington remained interested mostly in art and baseball.

Still, he was attracted to entertainment. As a boy he enjoyed putting on shows for his family. By twelve his interest had grown to the point where he was sneaking into burlesque shows, a popular theatrical entertainment form of the time. "The shows were very good," he recalled in his memoirs, "and I made a lot of observations, on show business techniques, on the great craftsmanship involved, and on the rather gorgeous girls."[9] He also began sneaking into a nearby poolroom, where he encountered a range of people from doctors to railway porters. He learned from this experience the value of mixing with a variety of humanity.

A third important factor in Ellington's education was the church. His father attended an African Methodist Episcopal (A.M.E.) Zion church, and his mother

Beyond the Ordinary

In his 1987 biography, Duke Ellington, *James Lincoln Collier remarks on Ellington's extremely close relationship with his mother.*

"The relationship between Ellington and his mother went beyond the ordinary. . . . Duke grew up secure in the unending love of his mother, a certitude [certainty] that he would always be first in her eyes. Few children are this lucky; and it left Duke with a sense that he was special. . . .

This view that he was special was cut into Duke's consciousness when he was very young, and it was to remain a salient [noticeable] element of his character for all his life. It manifested [showed] itself in his behavior in numberless ways: his refusal to scuffle in the muck with lesser men, even when they had badly wronged him; his ability to accept even the most fulsome [lavish] praise without a blush; his willingness to aspire to anything without fear; his commanding presence and ability to rule wherever he went."

Ellington (pictured at age four) enjoyed a happy and comfortable childhood. His parents constantly praised him, and always encouraged him in his endeavors.

was a Baptist. Young Edward went to church twice on Sundays—to both his mother's and his father's churches—and remained strongly religious all his life. He read the Bible regularly and later said that his three sacred concerts were the most important things he ever wrote. Each element in Ellington's upbringing was important, but he felt that his religious education was the most crucial. He once remarked, "I've had three educations—the street corner, going to school, and the Bible. The Bible is the most important. It taught me to look at a man's insides instead of the cut of his suit."[10]

Ellington's "three educations," along with his unwaveringly supportive family, played an important role in shaping his future. He grew up confident in his dealings with the world, secure in the knowledge that he could excel at anything. That anything would be music.

2 First Hints of Music

Every night I give a house party, and I'm the guest of honor.

—Duke Ellington on performing

When Ellington was young, recording was in its infancy. Radio, television, and talking pictures were still in the future. People made their own entertainment at home, often by singing and playing the piano. At the same time, many people rejected the strict morals of the Victorian era. A looser attitude about pleasure, which peaked with the Roaring Twenties, was taking shape. When new technology did arrive, a huge entertainment industry grew quickly to use it. As James Lincoln Collier noted, "It is no accident that the cabaret, the musical theater, the motion picture, the commercial music industry called Tin Pan Alley, the dance hall and the nightclub all developed as major institutions in the first two decades of [the twentieth] century."[11]

Several popular new forms of music were also evolving. Ragtime, which featured tricky time changes and complicated structures, was created in the late nineteenth century by black pianists around Saint Louis. The blues, which had originally come from the field songs of southern slaves, had evolved into a flexible and expressive song form. And jazz—a combination of ragtime, blues, church music, European concert music, improvisation, and other forms—was taking shape in New Orleans and other cities.

It is unlikely that young Edward heard much of this, at least at home; such music was considered low class by people of his family's standing. But in about 1912 a craze for social dancing swept America, featuring lively styles like the turkey trot, bunny hop, and slow drag; cabarets sprang up to accommodate the craze, which helped make the new music more acceptable.

Edward's one formal music course, in the spring of 1914, earned him a D. But by the time he was an adolescent, Edward was sneaking into dance halls like the True Reformer's Hall, Stack O'Lee's, and Murray's Casino. He was growing increasingly eager to learn piano, because, he always said, he could meet girls. He once remarked that he gave up baseball when he realized that "there was always a pretty girl standing down at the bass-clef end of the piano. I ain't been no athlete since."[12]

First Gigs

Edward began skipping school so he could hear famous pianists such as James P.

Johnson and Eubie Blake as they came to town. He also heard many locals, players with names like Blind Johnny and the Man with a Thousand Fingers. Ellington recalled later, "There were a lot of great piano players in Washington. Some of them were conservatory [music school] men and some of them played by ear, but one was always interested in what the other was doing. . . . It was a very good climate for me to come up in musically."[13]

A major influence was Doc Perry, a bandleader who taught Edward to read music. The boy's first paid musical job may have been filling in for Perry at an afternoon dance. He was also influenced by Harvey Brooks, a piano player he heard while on vacation in Atlantic City in 1913. Ellington later recalled, "He was swinging, and he had a tremendous left hand, and when I got home I had a real yearning to play. I hadn't been able to get off the ground before, but after hearing him I said to myself, 'Man, you're just going to *have* to do it.'"[14]

For his first gigs, or musical jobs, Edward played only other people's compositions, which he painstakingly learned by heart. Since he did not have a natural ear or much technique, he had to work hard to capture what others seemed to produce easily. He later said that this was what forced him to start writing. "I wasn't able to play what other composers wrote,

As Ellington reached his teens, a social dancing craze was sweeping America. In response, dance halls and cabarets began springing up all over the country.

so I had to create something that I could play. I remain a primitive artist, extremely primitive."[15]

In 1913, while working part-time as a soda jerk at the Poodle Dog Café, fourteen-year-old Ellington wrote his first piece. When the café's regular pianist showed up drunk, Edward took over—and thus was born the young musician's first original piece: "Soda Fountain Rag," also called "Poodle Dog Rag." It was based on the rhythms Ellington heard as he jerked soda water into ice-cream sodas. Ellington increased his repertoire, or supply of tunes, by changing the piece, making it a waltz or a fox-trot so that it sounded like a different tune.

This first effort was followed by another rag, "What You Gonna Do When the Bed Breaks Down?", a slow number that Ellington called "a pretty good hug-and-rubbin' crawl."[16] These early pieces, John Edward Hasse has pointed out, used everyday rhythms and other elements that Ellington later employed, including "listening to others, composing by playing, reworking memorable elements, and refining the piece in later performances. Composing and performing grew out of each other—even for fourteen-year-old Ellington."[17]

The Ellington Image

Even as a young man Ellington cultivated elegant manners. He carried himself as an aristocrat, inspiring self-confidence. William "Sonny" Greer, the drummer in Ellington's band for many years, recalled their first meeting: "From the moment I was introduced to Duke, I loved him. It was just something about him. . . . I've never seen another man like him. When he walks into a strange room, the whole place lights up."[18] Ellington carefully nurtured his larger-than-life image. One trick was to take his father's car at night, drive around, impress everyone, then refill the tank and let the engine cool before his father noticed.

Tinkering

Quoted in John Edward Hasse's Beyond Category, *Ellington had this to say about his first composition:*

"The only way I could learn how to play a tune was to compose it myself and work it up, and the first one was 'Soda Fountain Rag.'. . . I began by tinkering around with some old tunes I knew. Then, just to try something different, I set to putting some music to the rhythm that I used in jerking ice-cream sodas at the Poodle Dog. I fooled around with the tune more and more until at last, lo and behold, I had completed my first piece of finished music."

Ellington's stylish appearance, elegant manners, and aristocratic airs earned him the now-famous nickname Duke.

He also loved new clothes. Rex Stewart, later a member of Ellington's trumpet section, recalled, "One memorable evening Ellington astonished everybody by strolling up to the corner attired in a shimmy-back herringbone suit. . . . To all the style-conscious musicians, Duke was considered the epitome [height] of elegance from then on."[19] Ellington maintained a lifelong love of clothes; at one point, he reportedly owned 150 suits and 1,000 ties.

Ellington acquired his famous nickname from his lavish airs. In his memoirs, he wrote:

> I had a chum, Edgar McEntree . . . a rather fancy guy who liked to dress well. He was socially uphill and a pretty good, popular fellow around,

with parties and that sort of thing. I think he felt that in order for me to be eligible for his constant companionship I should have a title. So he named me Duke.[20]

The First Bands

By this time Ellington had expanded his musical horizons. At around the age of sixteen, he began rehearsing with a group of other young musicians at the True Reformer's Hall. Sometime in late 1917 or early 1918, Ellington joined his first official group. It had a changing array of players but usually included Ellington plus a drummer, a saxophonist, a banjo or guitar player, and sometimes a trumpeter. Years later he recalled the first paid date with this group at the True Reformer's Hall, on "the worst piano in the world. I played from 8 P.M. to 1 A.M. for 75 cents. Man, I snatched that money and ran like a thief. My mother was so proud of me."[21]

Though inexperienced, Ellington had little trouble finding work; there was always a demand for groups to play at dances. Sonny Greer, who had recently moved to Washington from New Jersey, was one of the band's founding members. Two others—trumpeter Arthur Whetsol and alto saxophonist Otto "Toby" Hardwick—would, like Greer, remain with Ellington for many years. Whetsol was sober and dependable; Hardwick had been a friend and neighbor of Ellington's since early childhood. When Hardwick first started performing with the group, he played string bass but was so little that his father had to carry the bass to his gigs for him.

Ellington (left) and drummer Sonny Greer in 1940. One of the band's founding members, Greer remained with Ellington's band for three decades.

Although the band was sometimes called the Duke's Serenaders, the leader was banjo player Elmer Snowden. They played rags, popular songs of the day like "Pretty Baby," instrumental dance tunes like waltzes and tangos, and a few originals. Their rehearsal room was in the True Reformer's Hall, only two blocks from the house Ellington lived in at 1212 T Street from ages eleven through seventeen. Even

---

An Artist from Birth

In this passage from his memoir, Duke Ellington in Person, *Mercer Ellington reflects on his father's early inclination to place art above mere accumulation of money.*

"He wasn't really a dud [at school], because his life could easily have run parallel to that of Einstein, whose grades, I understand, were terrible, too But what can definitely be said of Duke Ellington is that he was born an artist and that he had the typical way of an artist from birth. Basically, anything that didn't move or inspire him didn't exist, regardless of how it could be explained in philosophical terms. He understood the logic of money, that it was necessary to pay the rent and to procure food and clothing. He knew about it, but rather than attaching importance to it, he dismissed it, and this attitude was reflected throughout his life."

during rehearsals Duke was the center of attention. Rex Stewart recalled, "I can still see young Ellington playing the piano, and fixing that famous hypnotic smile on the nearest pretty girl."[22]

By March 1918 Ellington was feeling confident and increasingly independent. He moved out of his parents' house and into his own apartment. He got a telephone, still a luxury at the time, because he was listed as a musician in the classified section of the telephone book. This helped spread his reputation outside the black community, netting him a number of gigs at such places as the Women's Democratic Club.

In 1920 Greer was hired to play drums at the Howard Theater, the first large theater for black audiences in Washington. Through him, Ellington's band got a job playing predinner shows—one of five local bands that performed nightly. Occasionally they also played for open-air dances in parks or at indoor musical revues. It was an exciting environment, though sometimes frightening; the patrons of some clubs and bars were often full of liquor and ready for a fight. Rex Stewart recalled, "Of course, you had to know what the social climate might be before venturing into a hall where you were not known. . . . Sometimes you might have to leave a dance without your overcoat, your hat or even your head!"[23]

Marriage, Sign Painting, and Music

Duke had won a poster contest in 1916 sponsored by the National Association for the Advancement of Colored People (NAACP). The prize was a scholarship to the Pratt Institute of Applied Arts in Brooklyn, New York. But he became ineligible for it because he never graduated from high school. Attracted by the money and the social climate of entertainment, Ellington dropped out in early 1917, three months before graduation. To supplement his income, he started a poster and sign-painting company and, when the United States entered World War I, got messenger jobs with the Navy and the State Department. Ellington signed up for the draft in 1918 but was not called up. But the dance scene was exciting; the wartime crush of people in Washington meant plenty of work.

It was fortunate that Duke prospered at both sign painting and music, because by now he was a family man. He married a neighbor, Edna Thompson, in July 1918, and their son, Mercer Kennedy Ellington, was born the following March. A second

In 1918 Ellington married Edna Thompson, who was pregnant with their son Mercer. The couple's constant fighting and infidelities led to their separation in 1929, yet they remained officially married until Edna's death in 1966.

child was born later but did not live. Unfortunately the marriage was not a lasting one. Duke and Edna separated while Mercer was still small, although officially they remained married until her death in 1966. In Mercer's opinion, his parents had little in common and got married only because Edna was pregnant. "There was too much pulling them apart," Mercer was quoted as saying. "My mother's folks were from a higher station of black society than my father's. They were schoolteachers and principals, and they considered all musicians, including Duke Ellington, low-life."[24]

By 1919 Ellington could afford to buy his own car and house. But he realized that he needed to become a good businessperson if he was to truly succeed. The catalyst for this realization was a shocking experience: An older pianist, Louis Thomas, asked Ellington to play a solo gig at a fancy private party. Thomas told Ellington to collect $100, keep $10, and give him the remaining $90. Duke quickly realized that managing could be more lucrative than playing, and he wasted no time in becoming a booking agent. He took out a phone directory advertisement that announced, "IRRESISTIBLE JAZZ furnished to our select patrons: THE DUKE'S SERENADERS, COLORED SYNCOPATERS. E. K. ELLINGTON, MGR."

Duke soon learned many business tricks. For instance, he spoke quickly when people phoned him so that it sounded like he was in a hurry. He also tied his music

No Boxes

In Beyond Category, *John Edward Hasse points out that Ellington's early experiences gave him a hatred of categories.*

"His sister, Ruth, has said one of his mottoes was 'No boxes.' As Ellington disliked the way that black Washington maintained strata [class levels] based on income and pigmentation, he could only have chafed at the greater restrictions the white community placed on him, his family, and friends—restraints based solely on his racial category. And the way many of his teachers, performers, audiences, and venues would mix one kind of music with another probably led him to feel that the musical categories the larger society imposed had little meaning. Later, other experiences would intensify his aversion to categories, for example, the way people would limit their praise with the word 'Negro'; 'Ellington is a fine Negro composer.' The designations 'jazz musician' and 'jazz composer' served to restrict his music, and in later years he would speak out against such labels."

This is the earliest known picture of Ellington as a professional musician. It features Ellington (center) and Sonny Greer (left) during a 1918 stint at Louis Thomas's cabaret in Washington, D.C.

business to his sign painting. He recalled, "When customers came for posters to advertise a dance, I would ask them what they were doing about their music. When they wanted to hire a band, I would ask them who's painting their signs."[25] Soon Ellington was sending out as many as five bands a night under his name. The experience with Thomas had been valuable. For the rest of his life, Ellington controlled his own affairs as much as possible.

By the time the 1920s roared in, Ellington was a working musician. He was not yet a renowned composer and bandleader; he was a bright, restless young man who was trying to figure out his future. Chance played a big role in his path to music. If he had graduated from school, he would almost certainly have gone on to a career in visual art. If he had not been pressed for money, he might not have begun managing so aggressively and might not have sharpened the habits and skills that helped him to fame. But Ellington did take the path of performing—and changed American music forever.

3 Early Gigs

I had always considered myself a pretty suave guy. But Duke was more than suave. He had something special and he carried it with him all the time.

—Cab Calloway

Ellington and his friends had been itching for a chance to play in New York, then and now the world center for jazz musicians. Their desire for the big time became especially strong after Sonny Greer whetted their appetites with glamorous stories. Greer had grown up in New Jersey and had spent a little time playing in the big city. As he put it, "I was an authority, because my two aunts lived there and I had spent a good part of my schooldays in the city. I painted a glowing picture, a fabulous picture. We sat around drinking corn [whiskey] and telling lies, and I won the lying contest."[26]

A Taste of Harlem

In March 1923 Greer, Hardwick, and Ellington got their big break. They were asked to play a show in Harlem as part of Wilbur Sweatman's band. Sweatman was an old-fashioned vaudeville performer, whose specialty was playing three clarinets at the same time. The music was not jazz—it was much cornier than what such hip young musicians would have preferred—but they jumped at the chance. Ellington recalled, "Harlem, in our minds, did indeed have the world's most glamorous atmosphere. We had to go there."[27]

In the 1920s Harlem was the gathering place for Afro-Americans who craved intellectual, political, or cultural stimulation. Recent arrivals had made it one of the largest concentrations of black people in the country. In 1920 Harlem had seventy-three thousand residents in an area roughly twenty-five blocks long and six blocks wide. Important cultural figures such as poet Langston Hughes, social commentator and writer W. E. B. DuBois, and organizations such as the National Urban League were each contributing to the flourishing of black culture known as the Harlem Renaissance. In the words of writer James Weldon Johnson:

It [was] a Mecca for the sightseer, the pleasure-seeker, the curious, the adventurous, the enterprising, the ambitious, and the talented of the entire Negro world; for the lure of it has reached down to every isle of the Carib [Caribbean] Sea and penetrated even into Africa.[28]

At the same time, the entertainment world was exploding. Prohibition, the law that outlawed liquor in America, had gone into force in 1920 and would remain until 1933. It created a huge subculture of speakeasies, nightclubs where illegal liquor was sold. Every speakeasy had live entertainment; so did the neighborhood's many dance halls and theaters. So the music scene was jumping, and jobs playing in it were relatively easy to find.

The kings of Harlem's music world were pianists who played a style called stride. Stride was highly rhythmic and exciting; it featured a strong left hand, which kept up a rock-solid rhythm, while the right hand played showy runs. Stride piano players prided themselves on their ability to improvise, an important hallmark of jazz. In situations where a full band was impractical, a stride pianist could provide dance music all night long. Some of the kings of Harlem stride were Thomas "Fats" Waller, James P. Johnson, and Willie "the Lion" Smith. Stride knocked Ellington out, and its robust influence was evident for the rest of Ellington's career; he once remarked, with a straight face, "As Bach says, if you ain't got a left hand, you ain't worth a hoot in hell."[29]

Ellington also fell in love with Harlem. Where else could he eat the best food, flirt with the prettiest women, and hear the top piano players every night? He, Greer, and Hardwick vowed to stay in town after their week's run with Sweatman ended. However, this proved to be a more difficult task than they had thought. Work was

A vaudeville performance at Small's Paradise Club in Harlem. Harlem's entertainment industry was exploding in the 1920s, and Ellington's band jumped at the chance to play there.

Pianist Willie "the Lion" Smith made a name for himself in Harlem with his exciting, improvisational style of music known as stride. Ellington met Smith while in Harlem, and the two became lifelong friends.

not as easy to find as they had imagined. By day the trio hustled pool and by night went from club to club searching for jobs. They had to sleep at the homes of various relatives, and money was in short supply. At one point, Ellington claimed in later years, he and his friends were so poor that they had to split one hot dog three ways.

One thing that kept Ellington going during this rough spot was a friendship he formed with the great stride pianist Willie Smith. With his derby hat and cigar, Smith was a familiar figure in Harlem's music scene as well as a sought-after performer. Duke began tagging along with him on jobs; often, they would retire later to a friend's apartment to drink and play music until morning. Smith remained Ellington's friend for life and many years later gave a memorable performance at Duke's seventieth birthday party at the White House.

Besides club gigs, Smith also played at rent parties. These were private fund-raisers; they usually had an admission price of twenty-five cents to a dollar, and

Tripped Over

Writer Gene Lees, in his essay "The Enigma: Duke Ellington," notes Ellington's unusual method of orchestration.

"Duke didn't work that way. He put his colors together up through the sections, as it were, mixing and matching them in all sorts of odd ways. He was the first man in jazz . . . to use the wordless female voice as an instrumental color. . . . Whether Duke did it because one night he had only this possibility available to him or whether he planned it, I cannot say. Chances are that Duke found some of his combinations because of the vagaries [waywardness] of the band's behavior and then saw possibilities. . . . Many a great discovery is tripped over."

Ellington's band returned to Harlem for a lucky gig at Barron's Exclusive Club (pictured from across street), a fancy club that often catered to famous celebrities.

drinks cost a quarter. The profits went to pay the rent of whatever apartment was used for the party. As many as a hundred people might be jammed into a single apartment, and the parties often spilled out into the halls. Ellington and his crew soon began to rely on these rent parties to make a living. They knew that no matter how tough things were, they could look forward to making some money on Saturday nights. As Ellington once remarked, "In New York the gigs were few and far between, but [at rent parties] we could get all the food we wanted and take some home and a dollar besides."[30]

Finally, though, the constant hustle wore them down. As Ellington told the story, they found $15 in the street and used it to buy a meal and train tickets home. That way they could maintain the illusion to their friends and family that their conquest of the New York music scene had been thorough. As he put it, "'Course, all we need to have done was to send home and they would have sent us some money anyway, but we preferred to do it this way so we could make an entrance. You know,

'Just back from New York for a little holiday,' something like that."[31]

Barron's

Back in Washington, Ellington was reunited with his family and his sign-painting business. But a taste of New York had made him eager for more. Adding Snowden and Whetsol again to the trio, the group played briefly in Atlantic City and often had gigs around Washington. Then pianist and singer Fats Waller, whom the group had met in Harlem, recommended them to a New York vaudeville act he had performed with. They thought this would be another break for them. But when the five musicians arrived back in New York, in the summer of 1923, the deal had fallen through.

Fortunately, the band found another gig. Singer Ada "Bricktop" Smith was performing at a fancy Harlem nightspot called Barron's Exclusive Club. At Barron's the patrons dressed formally, were primarily white, and were often famous;

celebrities like baseball great Babe Ruth and New York's mayor, Jimmy Walker, were familiar sights there. Light-skinned blacks were grudgingly admitted if they were well-known or important personalities. Smith convinced the owner of Barron's that Ellington and his friends would fit the elegant mood. Better musicians were certainly available, but Ellington and his comrades had charm going for them: they were well-mannered, well-spoken, and conscientious.

They worked hard to maintain their high-class image at Barron's. Ellington recalled:

We paid quite a lot of attention to our appearance, and if any one of us came in dressed improperly Whetsol would flick his cigarette ash in a certain way,

or pull down the lower lid of his right eye with his forefinger and stare at the offending party. Whetsol was our first unofficial disciplinarian.[32]

They played mostly background music—corny, stilted society tunes. The money, however, made up for the lack of musical stimulation. Ellington recalled, "We used to get about thirty dollars apiece in tips every night, in addition to the salary . . . , which was real great."[33] Soon Duke felt confident enough to have Edna join him, though Mercer stayed in Washington with Ellington's parents.

That same summer a fancy "black and tan" called Connie's Inn opened in Harlem. A black and tan was a club that catered to both white and black audiences. Ellington got a job as a rehearsal pi-

"I Believe in the Personalities"

Ellington never had formal musical training. In an interview reprinted in Stanley Dance's The World of Duke Ellington, *he responds to the question, "Is a thorough musical education a help or a hindrance in jazz?"*

"There have been people who have come into jazz with no schooling and have become very famous, and there have been others with conservatory [music school] degrees who have also become very famous and done brilliant things. I think it's a good thing, no matter what kind of music you're in, to get all the training possible. It's necessary for some people to go to school to study. Perhaps they're already involved, doing it, and doing it very well. In their case, the limitations vary according to the personality. The whole thing is highly personal, anyway. Years ago, back in 1914, the people who were then identified with jazz had practically no training but they did some very wonderful and very interesting things. I believe in the personalities very strongly, in the great personalities of jazz."

anist for the stage shows there. This gave him a valuable education in putting together a successful musical revue. He also teamed up with a lyricist named Jo Trent to write popular songs, but they had little luck. Nor did Ellington have much success with recording. His group made its first record in July 1923, billed as Elmer Snowden and His Novelty Orchestra, but the disc was never issued.

The Private Ellington

Since childhood Ellington had always loved being the center of attention, and he always would. Now that he was in Harlem, he loved being in the middle of its swirl of creative activity. He also loved the increasing dominance, both musically and personally, that he was beginning to have within the band. He was a natural leader, and he was gradually taking control of the group.

Despite living his life more and more in public, however, Ellington remained an essentially private person. All his life Ellington maintained several different circles of friends, girlfriends, business associates, colleagues, and acquaintances. Although he dealt every day with a great many people, and he was constantly meeting new ones, he was careful to keep these circles separate.

During his early years as a musician in places like Barron's, Ellington began to refine the public persona, or image—one of complete charm and friendliness—that he used with these different groups of people. Over the years his outward shows of warmth became legendary. Despite the public displays of friendliness, however,

Ellington made sure that his personal life and emotions remained private. Max Jones, a British jazz writer who knew Ellington for many years, once remarked, "He was a most mysterious man. . . . I never understood him. Never got to any sort of comfortable place with him."[34] Record producer John Hammond recalled, "I never felt close to Duke as a person, and indeed, there were few who did. For all the up-front gregariousness . . . he was a very private person."[35] Even Ellington's wife, Edna, called him "a lonely man. He masks his emotions. Never wants you to know how he actually feels."[36]

Many other personal traits and habits that stayed with Ellington all his life were formed during these early professional years. He loved fine clothes, for instance, but hated anything that constricted or hindered his movement. He never wore a wristwatch, a belt, or shoelaces. He also hated ties, and whenever he had to wear one he always wore a large, soft collar so that he could not feel it. He had poor eyesight, but he was too vain to wear eyeglasses.

He also developed an impulsiveness in business decisions that did not always serve him well. Over the years many of his friends and associates advised him to look at the long-range picture in developing a career strategy. Ellington, however, remained interested only in what was happening at the moment; he cared nothing about the future or the past. Often he made decisions that served him well in the short term only, providing ready cash without regard to the next day. Biographer James Lincoln Collier put it this way: "With Ellington it was always *now*—this woman, this dish of pie and ice cream, this audience, this check, this orchestra, this piece of music."[37] This attitude extended to the point where he rarely wrote down full scores of his compositions and even to his refusal to make out a will.

The Hollywood Club

In September 1923 the group got its next big break. Elmer Snowden and His Black Sox Orchestra won what was supposed to be a six-month gig at a nightspot near Times Square called the Hollywood Club. The band was such a hit, however, that the engagement stretched to four years. This gig would prove to be the longest continuous engagement in Ellington's entire career.

The Hollywood was not a fancy club. Owned and managed by gangsters, as so many nightspots were during Prohibition, it was an after-hours club, one that opened at 11 P.M. to attract a late-night crowd. It was in a dingy basement, with a low ceiling and exposed pipes over the bandstand. The stage was so small that Duke's piano had to be put on the dance floor. The musicians called their dressing room the Black Hole of Calcutta. But what the Hollywood lacked in decor it made up for in liveliness, and it was a popular spot that often stayed open until sunrise. Sonny Greer recalled: "Our club was a little small place and after 3:00 in the morning you couldn't get a seat. They'd stand around and it got so popular, we were packed and jammed. . . . The floor was so crowded you couldn't dance."[38]

The band's outlook and style changed radically when it moved from Barron's to the Hollywood. For one thing, it took on a new name, the Washingtonians. More importantly, its music changed. The Hollywood's owners wanted to hear the exciting new sounds of hot jazz, not just polite background music.

The band also underwent its first major personnel change: Arthur Whetsol returned to school and was replaced by James "Bubber" Miley, a gifted trumpeter in the hot style of King Oliver and Louis Armstrong. To the muted plunger (wa-wa) effects that Oliver and Armstrong were pioneering, Miley added an earthy growl.

Ellington (top row, far right) and his band, the Washingtonians, in 1926. The band's popularity was on the rise, thanks in part to James "Bubber" Miley (bottom row, far right), a talented trumpeter with an electrifying style.

"From Elegant to Earthy"

Ellington rarely featured his own piano playing, preferring to spotlight the other players in the band. When he did, as John Edward Hasse points out in Beyond Category, *it was very special.*

"His piano sound was deep and resonant, his touch remarkable, his use of all registers of the piano exceptional. 'I have never encountered a pianist, jazz or classical,' [declared composer] Gunther Schuller, 'who could command at once such purity of tone *and* range of dynamics and timbres [tone quality] as Ellington.' His style was versatile, ranging from Harlem rent-shouts and down-home blues to poetic prefaces and impressionistic interludes, often laced with dissonant [discordant] clusters of notes. He could jump instantly from elegant to earthy. And as the years passed, his very personal piano playing became more creative and impressive."

Ellington was a dynamic and versatile pianist.

The result was electrifying. Although the group was still mostly playing stock arrangements of popular songs—that is, sheet music played straightforwardly as written—Miley's style set the Washingtonians apart. It gave the group a distinct style, more in keeping with the times than the corny music they had played at Barron's.

At the Hollywood the band began to mature musically. Although Ellington was not yet the leader, the Ellington sound was starting to take shape. Its distinctiveness is reflected in the band's first reviews. For instance, the New York newspaper the *Clipper* noted, "This colored band is plenty torrid [hot] and includes a trumpet player who . . . exacts the eeriest sort of modulations and 'singing' notes heard."[39] This "plenty torrid" band would soon be the talk of the town.

4 Breakthroughs

He was the greatest flirt—ever.

—Wynton Marsalis

Ladies and gentlemen—if you had seen her, you'd have understood.

—Duke Ellington, apologizing for arriving late on stage

Early in 1924 the band fired leader Elmer Snowden when they found he was taking more than his share of the money. In his memoirs, Ellington tells the story casually: "Elmer Snowden was the businessman of the group, and eventually he got so good at business that he went his way, and we had to get Freddy Guy to take his place."[40] But the departure also left the band without a leader. Ellington, with his knack for commanding and controlling, was a natural choice. It was a big job to lead a group of strong-willed men in an uncertain business, but Ellington was prepared to try. As he remarked later, "I told those guys . . . they were never going to drive me to the nuthouse. 'We may all go there,' I said, 'but I'm going to be driving the wagon.'"[41]

In March the Hollywood reopened as the Club Kentucky, also referred to as the Kentucky Club. It now featured both dancing and floor shows. In honor of Elling-

Ellington and his band at the popular Kentucky Club. When Ellington replaced Elmer Snowden (third from right) as the leader, the band was renamed Duke Ellington and His Club Kentucky Serenaders.

Ellington idolized Fletcher Henderson (far left), who led the country's top-ranked black band. Henderson was instrumental in developing the big band sound that swept America in the thirties.

ton's new status, the Washingtonians became Duke Ellington and His Washingtonians or Duke Ellington and His Club Kentucky Serenaders. By now an eight-piece group, it played for dancing and accompanied two shows nightly.

Top musicians as well as celebrities frequented the Kentucky and much of its popularity was due to Ellington's hot music. Author John Edward Hasse quotes the entertainment newspaper *Billboard:*

> If you must stay up until sunrise, we can't think, offhand, of a better place to while away the small hours than at the Club Kentucky. . . . Possessing a sense of rhythm that is almost uncanny, the boys in [the Ellington band] dispense a type of melody that stamps the outfit as the most torrid [hot] in town.[42]

Still, Ellington's band was not top dog. The number one white band in the country was Paul Whiteman's, and the cham-

pion black band was one led by Fletcher Henderson at the Roseland Ballroom. Henderson and his colleagues, including arranger Don Redman and Louis Armstrong, played an important role in inventing what later became the big band sound, which featured swinging rhythms and dueling reed and brass sections. Henderson was Ellington's idol. Duke once remarked, "When I first formed a big band in New York, his was the one I wanted mine to sound like."[43]

Side Gigs and Recording

While continuing its run at the Kentucky, the band played other gigs, including engagements at such well-known spots as the Cinderella Ballroom, Ciro's, and the Plantation Club. The band's size varied from session to session, and it often appeared under different names: Sonny Greer and

Years of Development

It took time for Ellington's skills to develop, according to Ellington scholar Mark Tucker in his liner notes to the CD collection Duke Ellington: The Blanton-Webster Band.

"Perhaps it's no more possible to account for the appearance of a Duke Ellington than to explain why there was a Mozart, a Leonardo, a Shakespeare. . . . On the other hand . . . if we turn away from the polished surface Ellington presented to the public and look more closely at the course of his career, we begin to see various stages of development. He was not always the great Duke Ellington. It took him years to rise in his profession and excel in his art. And although he gradually became proficient in a number of activities, he tended to acquire his skills at different times, at different rates of speed."

His Memphis Men, the Whoopee Makers, the Harlem Footwarmers, or the Six Jolly Jesters. Ellington had other jobs, too. He first tried his hand at a musical revue in the spring of 1925, teaming up with lyricist Jo Trent on *Chocolate Kiddies.* The show never made it to Broadway, but it ran in Harlem and toured Europe for two years, without Ellington. During the 1927-1928 season, the band backed three more revues, to which Ellington contributed some of the music: "Messin' Around," "Dance Mania," and "Jazzmania."

Ellington's recoding debut was in November 1924, when the band made the first recordings ever of Ellington compositions for the small Brunswick label. Later the group was able to record on major labels. In November 1926 at the first of these bigger sessions, the band recorded four Ellington compositions, including "East Saint Louis Toodle-Oo." This piece became a big hit, a jazz standard, and Ellington's theme song. "Toodle-Oo" (pro-

nounced toddle-oh) was, Ellington explained, a slang term for the limping way in which field-workers walked.

For many jazz musicians recording was simply a form of advertising. Ellington was one of the first to realize that records were not only promotional gimmicks but were, in fact, an entirely new medium. He began tailoring his compositions to fit a single-sided, ten-inch shellac record with a playing time of about three minutes. This meant packing as much variety as possible into a very short time. As John Edward Hasse notes, "To make a piece good for dancing at a performance, or listening once through, was one thing. But to make it listenable over and over again, via records, provided the composer a bigger challenge."[44]

Meanwhile, the band began appearing outside New York. There was no air-conditioning in the Club Kentucky, and the humid New York summers were virtually unbearable. To escape, the band began making annual tours of New England. Its first swing through the territories, as the musicians called any place outside New York City, came in the summer of 1924. These appearances, along with records, helped spread Ellington's popularity outside a small circle of New York musicians and jazz fans. One typical advance notice read: "Duke Ellington and His Washingtonians, Columbia and Brunswick Record Orchestra, Featuring Bub Miley, America's Hottest Trumpet Player."

Shaping the Sound

During the twenties Ellington began seriously working on his composition and arranging. Before, he had been content to play standard arrangements. But as his band began to ascend in popularity he realized that he needed to make his sound increasingly separate from run-of-the-mill dance music.

He was still happy to play pop tunes for dancing, but he also wanted to create something new: longer, semi-symphonic pieces that seriously reflected the lives of Afro-Americans. As Ellington put it in a magazine article:

> Our aim as a dance orchestra is not so much to reproduce "hot" or "jazz" music as to describe emotions, moods, and activities which have a wide range, leading from the very gay to the sombre. . . . [I look] to the everyday life and customs of the Negro to supply my inspiration.[45]

In 1927 the orchestra recorded the first of these pieces, *Black and Tan Fantasy* and *Creole Love Call.*

Just as he had earlier learned from Willie Smith, Ellington enlisted a couple of older men to help him. One was Will Vodery, the musical director for the Ziegfeld Follies, a famous Broadway revue. Another was Will Marion Cook, a classically educated violinist and composer. As Ellington recalled later of Cook: "He and I

Harry Carney (left) and Bubber Miley point out an advertisement for a coming engagement. The sign proclaims Ellington "the Paul Whiteman of colored orchestras."

would get in a taxi and ride around Central Park and he'd give me lectures in music. . . . He was a brief but strong influence."[46] Cook stressed individuality and originality: "First you find the logical way, and when you find it, avoid it, and let your inner self break through and guide you," he told Ellington. "Don't try to be anybody but yourself."[47]

Perhaps the most important step Duke took in shaping the Ellington sound was to discover the power of using individuals to contribute their best to the total sound. Since Bubber Miley's growling trumpet had been a hit, Ellington began nurturing the particular gifts of his other musicians. Everyone chosen for the band had a special strength, and Ellington would write music to fit each player like a glove. Alto saxophonist Johnny Hodges, who joined in 1928, was a prime example. Hodges had a gruff personality but a liquid, sensuous playing style. Some of Ellington's most beautiful pieces, such as "Warm Valley," were written specifically for Hodges.

Most bands of this era performed music that could be played by any competent musician. The star, typically, was the leader; the rest of the group was anonymous. The Ellington orchestra was different; separating the Ellington band from the Ellington sound was impossible. In fact, in later years some pieces were so closely identified with particular musicians that Ellington retired them as those players left. Writer Whitney Balliett once commented, "Most of the big bands that surrounded Ellington . . . came in two dis-

Celebrating Differences

In this excerpt from his essay "The Enigma: Duke Ellington," Gene Lees discusses Ellington's love of the eccentric.

"He took the world as he found it, both in life and in music, tolerating discrepancies and contradictions in men and circumstance. That is how he was able to make a functioning unit of men with such disparate [different] sounds and personalities. Therein lies one difference between classical and jazz composition. Classical music assumes, within a certain narrow variability, a 'correct' trumpet sound or a 'correct' trombone sound. Jazz tolerates all sorts of peculiarity, and Duke went beyond toleration: he celebrated difference. He turned idiosyncrasies to advantage and accommodated Ray Nance's violin; Cat Anderson's paper-thin high-note trumpet; the swooping golden-sad alto saxophone of Johnny Hodges; the big throaty baritone saxophone of Harry Carney . . . and the smoky autumnal trombone of Lawrence Brown."

tinct parts—their leaders . . . and the disposable hired help. But Ellington and his musicians were indivisible."[48]

Ellington hired men who were not big names because stars were expensive and because he liked molding fresh players. But he always chose ones with distinctive sounds and individual personalities. As Balliett put it, "Ellington was a brilliant eccentric who attracted brilliant eccentrics."[49] Writing for them involved a form of psychology: Ellington had to get to know a player well, musically and otherwise. He once remarked, "You can't write music right unless you know how the man that'll play it plays poker."[50]

New Players

Besides Hodges, a number of other key players came on board during the 1920s. Joe "Tricky Sam" Nanton, famous for the wide range of sounds he coaxed from his trombone, joined in 1926 and remained until his death twenty years later. Also joining around this time were valve trombonist Juan Tizol, a native of Puerto Rico, and two New Orleans musicians, bassist Wellman Braud and clarinetist Barney Bigard.

Bigard, with his rich tone and fluid style, became an especially crucial part of Ellington's sound palette. At first reluctant to leave Luis Russell's successful band, Bigard was nonetheless attracted by Ellington's regard for individuals. As Bigard recalled:

I noticed he kept talking in the plural: "Our band," "We can stay there," and I liked that from the start about him. He thought of the band as a unit. . . . Duke Ellington made you feel so

Band members (clockwise from far left) Johnny Hodges, Barney Bigard, Harry Carney, and Otto "Toby" Hardwick. Ellington recruited players with unique sounds, and wrote music that brought out the best in each.

much at ease. Just like he was going to turn the music business upside down and you would be part of it.[51]

The clarinetist ended up staying for fourteen years.

Another musician who would spend many years with Ellington was baritone saxophonist Harry Carney. Carney was only seventeen when he joined in 1927 and was still with the band when Ellington died in 1974, making his stay the longest tenure of any other Ellington musician. The big baritone sax is difficult to play gracefully, but Carney was a master. As Mercer Ellington wrote of Carney, "His massive tone not only gave the saxophone section a depth and roundness no other had, but it gave the whole ensemble a rich sonorous [resounding] foundation that proved inimitable [impossible to imitate]."[52]

But the band also suffered its first major loss—trumpeter Bubber Miley, who was a heavy drinker. More and more Miley was showing up for gigs after partying all night, and eventually he started not showing up at all. In 1929 Charles "Cootie" Williams, the classically trained son of an Alabama minister, stepped in to fill his place.

As Ellington tightened his band and perfected his sound, he asserted himself more and more as a leader. Soon it was clear that the Ellington orchestra was an all-star band but that Ellington was the chief star; now it was truly Duke Ellington and His Orchestra. As Otto Hardwick remarked about rejoining the band after an absence, "It wasn't *our* thing any longer. It had become Ellington's alone. This was in-evitable, I guess. Ten years ago it was '*We* do it this way' and '*We* wrote that.' Now, the we was *royal*."[53]

The band that would put Duke Ellington on top was, more or less, in place. As James Lincoln Collier put it, "Ellington had finally put together the musical instrument with which he would create some of the finest jazz ever played and on which he could climb to fame."[54] The band was stable over the next decade; new players were added, but few dropped out. This was a remarkable achievement in the world of jazz, where groups form and dissolve with speed and regularity.

"They'll Drink *Anything*!"

Ellington once told Stanley Dance, in an interview reprinted in Dance's book The World of Duke Ellington, *his feelings about the wrong and right ways of listening to music.*

"People are told that they must never drink anything but a white wine with fish or a red wine with beef. The people who don't know, who've never been told that, who've never been educated along those lines—they'll drink *anything!* I suspect they get as much joy out of their eating and drinking as the other people.

It's just like people who listen to music. They don't necessarily *know* what they're listening to. They don't have to know that a guy is blowing a flatted fifth or a minor third, but they enjoy it, and this I consider healthy and normal listening. A listener who has first to decide whether this is proper form when a musician plays or writes something—that's not good. It's a matter of 'How does it sound?' and, of course, the sound is modified by the taste of the listener. . . .

Music itself is a category of sound, but everything that goes into the ear is not music. Music is music, and that's it. If it sounds good, it's good music, and it depends on who's listening *how* good it sounds!"

Irving Mills

While Ellington was fine-tuning his orchestra, he made another move designed to further his career: he acquired a manager. Irving Mills was an intelligent, fast-talking white native of New York who in 1919 had started a successful music publishing company. Mills Music was famous for finding and publishing unknown but gifted songwriters who would later become stars, including Harold Arlen and Hoagy Carmichael.

But Mills was interested in branching out into management as well as publishing. Ellington's first record on a major label, for Vocalion, was arranged by Mills after he had heard the band at the Kentucky Club. The management deal Mills and Ellington struck was between the two of them, not between Mills and the band, and this move helped cement Ellington's status as the band's leader.

Mills insisted that Ellington record his own pieces almost exclusively, rather than including popular tunes written by others. In part this was because the Ellington sound was more distinctive, but no doubt it was also because Mills, the publisher, and Ellington, the composer, both made more money with originals. This helped Mills, of course, but it also let Ellington earn money and gain business experience while furthering his artistic goals as a composer. As John Edward Hasse wrote:

> This particular confluence [joining] of art and commerce, artist and entrepreneur, black and white would come to greatly enrich twentieth-century culture. And too, it increased the intimate interrelationship and mutual interde-

As Ellington's manager, Irving Mills worked tirelessly promoting the band. His efforts paid off; Ellington became famous, and both men became wealthy.

pendency of Ellington's two careers [as composer and bandleader].[55]

Mills was tireless. He browbeat radio stations, badgered record companies, and traveled regularly with the orchestra. Sonny Greer recalled: "When anything important pertaining to Ellington came up, [Mills] was there in person. . . . When he made the second European trip with us, he was so sick he had to have a doctor in attendance twenty-four hours a day, but he made it every step of the way."[56]

It was crucial in those times for a black musician to have a white manager, because it was impossible for the musician to be taken seriously or with respect without backup from a powerful white manager. Many have criticized this arrangement, but the simple truth was that it was neces-

"Her Every Gesture"

In his memoirs,
Music Is My
Mistress, *Ellington*
explains the book's
title and reflects that,
for him, music was a
lifelong love affair.

"I have a mistress. Lovers have come and gone, but only my mistress stays. She is beautiful and gentle. She waits on me hand and foot. She is a swinger. She has grace. To hear her speak, you can't believe your ears. She is ten thousand years old. She is as modern as tomorrow, a brand-new woman every day, and as endless as time. . . . Living with her is a labyrinth of ramifications. I look forward to her every gesture.

Music is my mistress, and she plays second fiddle to no one."

sary in those days if the artist was to succeed. Ellington had Irving Mills and Louis Armstrong had Joe Glaser; both musicians became rich and famous. On the other hand, some brilliant musicians such as Jelly Roll Morton and King Oliver were never represented by white managers. But as James Lincoln Collier has noted, "they died penniless and virtually forgotten. The equation was as simple as that."[57]

The arrangement between Mills and Ellington was mutually beneficial. They both became wealthy, Ellington became famous, and—most importantly—Ellington could concentrate on music, rather than on the day-to-day problems of leading a band. All his life Ellington hated hassles, and Mills provided a buffer between Duke and the rest of the world. As Barney Bigard recalled, "We musicians never ever got involved. Mills would fix a deal and tell Duke, and then Duke would tell the band. There was never any doubt about who had the band though. We were working for Duke and not for Irving Mills."[58]

Ellington's skills as a composer and arranger were blossoming. He had assembled a crack band, one with a unique overall sound as well as a variety of distinctive individuals. He also had the final piece of the puzzle—a good manager. After an uncertain beginning to Ellington's New York career, things were looking up. The stage was set for stardom.

5 The Heart of Harlem

If I am asked to describe New York, I must think in musical terms, because New York is people, and that is what music is all about. This incredible city embraces all humanity within its structure, whether resident or visitor, and joins each new heartbeat with her own throbbing pulse.

—Duke Ellington

Harlem had the best nightclubs in the world, and the cream of the crop was the Cotton Club. Up to seven hundred people could be served in this elegant spot by red-tuxedoed waiters. The club was lavishly, if bizarrely, decorated: log cabin outside, jungle inside, Southern plantation for the bandstand. The clientele was almost completely white, though blacks were allowed in if they were important figures.

All the entertainers were Afro-American. Elaborate floor shows featured singers, dancers, comedians, and chorus girls in costumes that changed with every number. These revues were crazy assemblies that made little sense but always entertained. A new show with material from staff composers and writers opened every six months.

It is unclear how Ellington's relatively new band got the plum job of backing the Cotton Club revue. Jimmy McHugh, a songwriter for the club, says he convinced the club's management to sign Ellington. According to Ellington, however, Irving Mills arranged an audition while the band was in Philadelphia in the fall of 1927. Ellington hurried back, frantically rounded up extra players to make the sound fuller, and was two hours late for the audition. Fortunately the club's manager was also late.

In any event, the club's owner, gangster Owney Madden, wanted Ellington to start right away, but Ellington had to finish his run in Philadelphia. According to legend, Madden sent a man named Yankee Schwarz to see the owner of the Philadelphia club. Schwarz told him, "Be big, or be dead." The club owner decided to be big about it and released Ellington from the contract.

At first the band, which expanded when it got the Cotton Club gig, sounded rough, due to a combination of unfamiliar music, new members, and little rehearsal time. Once these opening problems were solved, however, the band was a hit. As the national entertainment newspaper *Variety* commented at the time, "In Duke Ellington's dance band, Harlem has reclaimed its own."[59] Ellington, a natural showman and a lover of artifice, or artfulness, fit perfectly into the fantasy world of the

A 1930 publicity photo of Ellington's orchestra during their engagement at the exclusive Cotton Club. The band was a huge hit with audiences at this lavish nightclub.

Cotton Club's revues. His unusual and exotic style was custom-made for it. The band's Cotton Club engagement, in fact, proved to be a pivotal moment in American music: many historians feel it perfectly represents the essence of the Jazz Age.

Radio, Films, Broadway

The stock market crash of 1929 devastated the nation's economy and ushered in the Great Depression, which lasted well into the thirties. Musicians everywhere were hit hard, but Ellington's was one of the few orchestras that flourished.

In part this was because it was already established on radio. In 1927 the band had begun broadcasting nationally on CBS. The medium was still new, and Ellington was one of the first black bandleaders to try it. He was thus well positioned when radio proved to be enormously influential and popular. As

John Edward Hasse put it, "Radio transformed American life, creating instantaneous common experiences throughout the vast nation . . . and reducing the public's need to create its own entertainment at home."[60]

Ellington's live radio shows from the Cotton Club became legendary. By May 1930 the band was broadcasting five or six nights a week, at dinnertime and again late at night for West Coast reception. Ellington was one of the first composers to write a piece, "Dreamy Blues," specifically to take advantage of microphone transmission and broadcasting. He received so much fan mail about the tune that he refined it into the classic "Mood Indigo." The timid radio industry and its sponsors, however, refused to give Ellington a show of his own. A Bridgeport, Connecticut, *Herald* writer editorialized, "I do not think I am telling any stories out of school when I submit that the reason such great names as Ellington and [Cab] Calloway haven't profited commercially in radio is because

The Cotton Club Spirit

Singer and bandleader Cab Calloway, who nearly rivaled Ellington's popularity in the 1930s, comments in his memoirs, Of Minnie the Moocher and Me, *on the Cotton Club rehearsals.*

"It is no accident that the name Cotton Club has come to be synonymous with the greatest Negro entertainment of the Twenties and Thirties. A lot of people worked hard as hell to pull those shows together. . . . That was the Cotton Club spirit. Work, work, work. Rehearse, rehearse, rehearse. Get it down fine. Tops and professional in every sense of the word. The club was alive with music and dancing at night, but it was also alive all day long. If the chorus line wasn't rehearsing, then the band was. We knew we were performing before some of the most critical audiences in the world. We knew we had a standard of performance to match every night. We knew we couldn't miss a lick. And we rarely did."

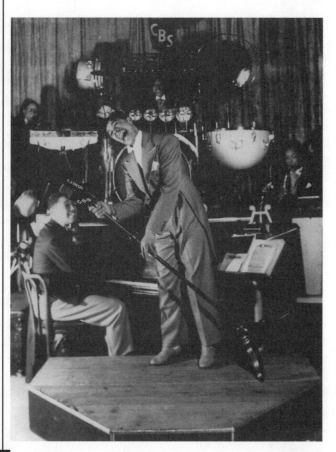

Cab Calloway performs at the Cotton Club in 1935. The club became famous for its top-notch entertainment in the 1920s and 1930s.

national sponsors steer clear of arousing Southern race prejudices. Too bad."[61]

The first full-length movie with sound, *The Jazz Singer*, had caused a sensation in 1927, and in 1929 Ellington got a shot at the talkies when the band recorded *Black and Tan Fantasy*, a nineteen-minute short. The next year the band went to Hollywood to appear in a feature starring the comics Amos and Andy. The movie industry was almost completely segregated at this time, and Amos and Andy were actually white actors in blackface, or makeup. For the Ellington band's scene, the producers even forced Juan Tizol, a Hispanic, and Barney Bigard, a light-skinned Creole, to wear blackface!

Band members (left to right) Hardwick, Carney, Bigard, and Hodges at the Cotton Club. The band's frequent live radio broadcasts from the club kept them popular and profitable despite the country's tough economic times.

Back in New York in 1930, the band returned to the Cotton Club and appeared in the Broadway revue *Show Girl*, which featured such famous performers as comedian Jimmy Durante and dancer Ruby Keeler; the music was by George Gershwin. Ellington's band had a plum position, appearing onstage, rather than in the orchestra pit as usual, and performing their greatest hits. *Show Girl* was a tremendous success, and soon the band was receiving the huge sum of $1,500 a night.

On the Road

As if Ellington's Cotton Club, Broadway, radio, and recording work was not enough, Mills also arranged for a series of out-of-town engagements. The band's fame had spread far enough to justify touring, and it spent much of 1931 on the road.

The tour concentrated on the Midwest. Musically it was important because Ellington acquired his first featured singer. Until now, except for singers in Cotton Club shows, Ellington had relied only on the occasional vocals of Sonny Greer and Cootie Williams. But in Chicago he hired Ivie Anderson, who stayed for eleven years. Anderson popularized many of Duke's best songs, such as "It Don't Mean a Thing (If It Ain't Got That Swing)." She had an attractively smoky voice and an angelic stage presence, as she was usually dressed in white. According to Rex Stewart, however, she had a salty side and was always "bossing the poker game, cussing out Ellington, playing practical jokes, or giving some girl advice about love and life."[62]

Singer Ivie Anderson joined Ellington's band in 1931. Her sultry vocals added a new element to Ellington's sound, and helped to popularize many of his best songs.

Ellington was a huge success in the Midwest. The Chicago *American* raved:

> His is a band that really entertains. The program he presents is swift moving. . . . The wah wah cornetist, trombonist and other instrumentalists were so eloquent, indeed, during the performance we attended that the audience would not stop applauding some of the numbers for many minutes.[63]

The band returned to Chicago five times in 1931 alone, breaking box office records and paving the way for black artists to play venues in Chicago that had previously been open only to white performers.

Ellington was also a hit with many serious composers. At one point he was invited to lecture at Columbia University, where the classical music professors raved about him. Composer Percy Grainger, chairman of the music department at New York University, compared Ellington's

"So Much Goes On"

In a 1944 magazine interview reprinted in Mark Tucker's Duke Ellington Reader, *Ellington describes the inspiration for his piece "Harlem Air Shaft."*

"So much goes on in a Harlem air shaft. You hear fights, you smell dinner, you hear people making love. You hear intimate gossip floating down. You hear the radio. The air shaft is one great big loudspeaker. You see your neighbor's laundry. You hear the janitor's dogs. The man upstairs' aerial falls down and breaks your window. You smell coffee. A wonderful thing, that smell. An air shaft has got every great contrast. One guy is cooking dried fish and rice and another guy's got a great big turkey. . . . You hear people praying, fighting, snoring. Jitterbugs are jumping up and down always over you, never below you. . . . I tried to put all that in 'Harlem Air Shaft.'"

genius for melodic invention to Bach's. In fact Ellington rarely listened to other composers or even to his own recordings; he was too interested in current sounds, he said, to worry about the past. When told once that a critic had compared him to Strauss and Stravinsky, Ellington replied, "Hot damn! I guess that makes me pretty good, doesn't it?"[64]

Such attention from so-called serious music composers and critics encouraged Ellington to keep writing compositions beyond the standard jazz and pop boundaries. Early in 1931 the band recorded the ambitious *Creole Rhapsody*. It was much longer than usual, taking up two sides of a 78-rpm (revolutions per minute) record and running about six and a half minutes. In 1932 the piece won the prestigious New York Schools of Music Award for the best new work by an American composer.

Keeping the Band Together

The group Ellington had on the road was the nucleus of what would become the longest continuously operating big band in the history of jazz. Part of his leadership role meant learning to keep his musicians in order. Considering their wildly different personalities, and considering how often jazz musicians usually join or leave groups, he did a remarkable job. There were relatively few changes in the band's personnel compared with its long life, and many of its members stayed for

Ellington's ability to keep his players happy and musically challenged helps to explain why many of them stayed with the band for decades.

decades. Keeping them happy required a complex set of maneuvers. Ellington used a combination of psychological tactics, constant promises of more money, smooth talking, and professional flattery to maintain the peace.

In some ways the band remained notoriously loose in its work habits. Ellington often had to play long piano introductions to pieces in order to give the rest of the musicians time to filter back onstage after an intermission. Ellington himself had little regard for schedules. An influential black newspaper, the *Afro-American*, once remarked, "It is no secret among theater folk that the Duke is one of the most irresponsible men in show business. Whenever he is playing an engagement one or two of his bandsmen follow him around to make sure he gets on the stage on time."[65]

In other ways the group was a tightly run organization. They used their tip money, for instance, to set up a fund to pay for new uniforms. Players were fined a dollar for every fifteen minutes they were late for a gig or rehearsal, and this money also went into the fund. A musician who did not show up at all without advance notice, forfeited a whole night's pay. And Ellington could be ruthless about maintaining the quality of musicianship. He rarely fired players over the years, but he was a master at making life so difficult for an offending individual that he inevitably quit.

As might be expected with any long-lasting organization, not everything worked smoothly all the time. Feuds between players were common and could last for years. Sometimes these erupted into public battles. On one occasion two players got into a fight while performing, and they chased each other around and off the stage. Smoothly, Ellington announced to the audience that they had just witnessed part of a new act. Afterwards he did not yell at the musicians; instead, he merely remarked that if they wanted to fight again, they should let him know so that he could write some music to go with it.

Some members of the band also loved to play pranks on each other, especially as a way of staying amused during long tours. One favorite involved putting cayenne pepper or Limburger cheese into a mouthpiece left onstage by a trumpeter or trombonist. Another was to tie together the shoelaces of a musician in the back row who was quietly trying to sleep off a hangover, then yell "FIRE!" and watch the hapless man try to get to his feet. Still another joke was to put itching powder in someone's band uniform. Almost anything was acceptable in the constant battle against boredom on the road.

Personal Life

Ellington's professional star was on the rise, but his personal life was chaotic. His marriage to Edna was deteriorating, even though their son had moved from Washington to join them. Both had outside affairs, and they fought constantly. Edna slashed Duke's face on one occasion, probably with a razor, and the scar remained for the rest of his life. In his memoirs, Ellington mischievously wrote that he had four stories about it:

> One is a taxi-cab accident; another is that I slipped and fell on a broken bottle; then there is a jealous woman; and last is old Heidelberg, where they used to stand toe to toe with a saber in each

Cotton Club dancer Mildred Dixon moved in with Ellington in 1929 after his separation from Edna. Their relationship was not a long-lasting one.

hand, and slash away. The first man to step back lost the contest, no matter how many times he'd slashed the other. Take your pick.[66]

The couple separated in 1929 and Ellington's new sweetheart, Mildred Dixon, moved into his apartment in Sugar Hill, a prestigious Harlem neighborhood. Mildred, a Cotton Club dancer, was so petite compared to the imposing Ellington that he gave her the ironic nickname Tubby. In a typical attempt to avoid controversy, Ellington did not tell his family of the changes. Mercer Ellington recalled, "I came home from school one day, and there was a strange woman living with my father. . . . They [Duke and Edna] had separated without telling us. Nobody in my family liked to be the bearer of bad news."[67]

In 1930 Ellington brought his mother, father, and sister from Washington to live with him. J. E. was reluctant, but Daisy insisted. Ellington's proud father grudgingly accepted a make-work job answering the hundreds of fan letters a day that his son received. Now Duke truly controlled his family; everyone was dependent on him. James Lincoln Collier has remarked that the arrangement was unusual:

> It was not an idea that would have occurred to every man in Duke's position. He was a celebrity, he was making money, he had a virtually unlimited supply of women available to him, and he liked the fast life. Why encumber himself with a mother who had Victorian ideas about sin and a kid sister who could not be exposed to the sort of life the Cotton Club epitomized?[68]

But Ellington always had an unusual relationship with his family. Though his personal life was chaotic, he was trying to control those elements he could. Soon, he would encounter even greater heights and depths.

6 Fame and Change

You know, Stan Kenton can stand in front of a thousand fiddles and a thousand brass and make a dramatic gesture and every studio arranger can nod his head and say, "Oh, yes, that's done like this." But Duke merely lifts his little finger, three horns make a sound, and I don't know what it is.

—André Previn, composer and conductor

During the depression record sales dropped and the Ellington band survived only by touring constantly in its own railroad cars. These cars were efficient transport, provided an alternative to finding hotels that accepted blacks, and created good publicity when they pulled into a new town. Ellington loved trains, partly because he hated to be rushed. On a train he could not be hurried.

Besides making a living, touring gave Ellington a chance to connect with black communities beyond Harlem, where he was a hero. Novelist Ralph Ellison, then a young boy in Oklahoma, was profoundly inspired by Ellington's depression-era visits.

Ellington and his orchestra receive a warm welcome upon their arrival in Los Angeles in 1934. The band toured constantly throughout the thirties, and everywhere the reception was overwhelmingly positive.

"A Sort of Secret Society"

Writer Gene Lees, in his essay "The Enigma: Duke Ellington," reflects on the odd amalgam, or combination, of people called the Duke Ellington Orchestra.

"They were a strange sort of traveling circus that Duke somehow knew how to handle, men who in some cases couldn't fit anywhere else in musical society but whose idiosyncrasies of sound Duke could use as colors in his own highly personal tapestries. He said he stayed on the road because it gave him the privilege of hearing his own music every night, but it is reasonable to suspect he also did it to provide employment for his orphans. His ASCAP [American Society of Composers, Authors, and Publishers] earnings from his songs must have been enormous, so he didn't have to do it for the money.

His band was a sort of secret society whose members did as they pleased, and Duke let them get away with it. 'But when it really matters,' he once [said], 'they came through for me.' Indeed they did."

He later wrote that the band members "were news from the great wide world, an example and a goal."[69] Everywhere the band was warmly received. On its first visit to Los Angeles, for instance, the group was greeted by hundreds of fans who formed an impromptu parade and escorted the orchestra to its hotel.

Ellington always tried to play a variety of places because he liked the change of pace. He once remarked, "I've always preferred to mix dances and concerts, to play high-brow stuff in the concert hall . . . and the next night to play a prom."[70] But dances were his staple, and they were typically a mixture of informal fun and big-city sophistication. A crowd would gather around the stage, intently watching Ellington in his tuxedo and the musicians in their white uniforms and crimson bow

ties. Things kicked off with a fast tune like "Ring Dem Bells," followed by a mix of Ellington originals and pop hits. The wise-cracking Sonny Greer and the ultra-smooth Ellington took turns announcing. Ivie Anderson sang, without a microphone, numbers like "It Don't Mean a Thing" or "Minnie the Moocher." And the crowd danced like crazy.

For years Ellington resisted traveling in the deep South, fearful of bigotry. Singer Cab Calloway had been the first person to take an all-black big band there, in 1931, and it had been a humiliating, dangerous experience. In 1933 Ellington decided the time was right. His tour began in Dallas, where he broke box office records, and the Dallas *News* enthused, "This is not butterfly jazz with three months' life. It can and probably will be performed whenever you can find musicians to play it."[71] The band also played, with no major incidents, through the rest of the deep South at separate dances for whites and blacks.

Southern racism was no joke, but sometimes it was more funny than frightening. At one point the band needed to eat, and Ellington recruited Barney Bigard, a Creole—that is, a Louisiana native who has mixed Afro-American, French, and Spanish ancestry—to bring food out of a restaurant, because Bigard was the whitest looking member of the band. After a long time Bigard came back outside, shouting, "I'm Creole! I'm Creole!" The white restaurant owner followed him out on the porch, shouting back, "I don't care *how* old you are, you can't eat in here!"

To Europe

In the summer of 1933 the band made a fifty-five-day tour of England, Holland, and France. Some American jazz musicians had settled in Europe, but only a few major players had toured there. Only a small group of European fans knew about jazz, and Ellington's tour was one of their first opportunities to appreciate it live.

The band crossed the Atlantic on an ocean liner. When he heard that the ship was steered by automatic pilot at night, Ellington—who was always superstitious—resolved to stay up all night. He did not trust the ship to avoid the icebergs that were surely waiting for him. He spent the nights playing cards or pacing the deck, sleeping only when a human pilot could take over. Ellington was superstitious in other ways. He never accepted or gave gifts of shoes, since that meant the other person would walk away from him. He hated the color green because it reminded him of graves, and brown because he was wearing a brown suit the day his mother died. And thirteen was his lucky number because he had once opened a successful engagement on Friday the thirteenth.

On arrival in London the band discovered a double standard for blacks. On the one hand they were met by a huge crowd of adoring fans and eager reporters. On the other hand they had difficulty finding lodging that would accept them. Ellington, as befitted his star status, stayed at the elegant Dorchester Hotel, but the rest of his eighteen-person party had to find lesser hotels and rooming houses.

On the whole, however, the admiration and respect the orchestra received balanced any prejudice. Its two-week run at the Palladium, the world's foremost vaudeville theater, was standing room only. A new box office record was set the first day. According to Ellington, that first performance "scared the devil out of the whole band. The applause was so terrifying—it was applause beyond applause."[72]

This response symbolized the enthusiasm English jazz fans had for the music. The band was astonished to find fans who knew more about details of recording dates than they did themselves. Ellington recalled, "We couldn't understand how people in Europe, who heard us only through the medium of records, could know so much about us."[73] British critics, however, were mixed in their reception of the new music from abroad. One called Ellington "the first composer of uncommon merit, probably the first composer of real character, to come out of America,"

Ellington's orchestra played to a standing-room-only crowd during their two-week engagement at the London Palladium. The band was amazed at the number and enthusiasm of English jazz fans.

while another called him "a Harlem Dionysus, drunk on bad bootleg liquor."[74]

While in London, Ellington met a royal fan: the Prince of Wales, later King Edward VIII. The prince, an amateur drummer, asked to sit in during a jam session at a reception. Ellington recalled: "The Prince of Wales wanted to show Sonny how to beat those drums. We expected some Little Lord Fauntleroy stuff, but he really gave out some low-down Charleston."[75] The band was received equally warmly when it continued on to Holland and France. Such treatment was, of course, exactly to Ellington's liking, and he was reluctant to leave Europe. He later commented, "The main thing I got in Europe was *spirit*. That kind of thing gives you the courage to go on. If they think I'm *that* important, then maybe . . . our music does mean something."[76]

Changes

The European trip rejuvenated Ellington's creative drive, and soon afterwards he wrote two of his most famous songs, "In My Solitude" and "In a Sentimental Mood," as well as such classic pieces as "Jive Stomp," "Rude Interlude," and "Daybreak Express." But then came a terrible blow. His mother was diagnosed with cancer in the fall of 1934 and passed away the following spring. Ellington, devastated but determined to honor her, ordered for the funeral three thousand flowers and a casket that cost $3,500—at a time when most American families lived on less than $2,000 a year. Barney Bigard recalled that the only time he knew Ellington to miss a job was when Duke attended Daisy's funeral. The replacement pianist "did a fine job," Bigard wrote, "but the band wasn't the same. Everyone in the band knew they were working with a genius [Ellington]."[77]

Another blow came as Ellington's father's drinking, which had always been a problem, became severe. In 1937 J.E. died of a lung disease, pleurisy, aggravated by alcoholism. Ellington's world had revolved around his parents, especially his mother, and now they were both gone. Many people who knew Ellington say he never fully recovered from the loss.

For months he wallowed in a deep depression, recording little and writing virtually nothing. On some days he did little but weep. Gradually, however, the grief slackened and Ellington was able to write a new piece dedicated to his mother, *Reminiscing in Tempo*. Released on two 78s, it was his most ambitious composition yet. Unfortunately, it was poorly received. John Hammond, an influential jazz producer and writer, called it "arty" and "pretentious." Such reactions stung Ellington and probably stifled his still-tentative feelings about serious concert music.

Late in 1937 Ellington met someone who helped fill the void left by the deaths of his parents. Dr. Arthur C. Logan, eleven years Ellington's senior, would become

"Like a Giant Pulse"

In his 1944 profile of Ellington, reprinted in Mark Tucker's Duke Ellington Reader, New Yorker *writer Richard O. Boyer describes a typical performance.*

"In general, or so its members like to think, the more exhausted the Ellington band is, the better it plays. Ordinarily, the tempo at the beginning of a dance is rather slow; both players and dancers have to warm up to their interdependent climax. By midnight both are in their stride. Then the trumpets screech upwards in waves, sometimes providing a background for a solo, soft and sensuous, by tough little Johnny Hodges, alto saxophonist, who advances toward the front of the stage threateningly and who holds his instrument as if it were a machine gun with which he is about to spray the crowd. . . . Junior Raglin's bass fiddle beats dully, like a giant pulse. Junior's eyes are closed and his face is screwed up as if he were in pain. Duke's face is dominated by an absorbed, sensual scowl as he plays his piano. Sonny [Greer], a cigarette waggling before an impassive face, jounces up and down on his stool so hard that he seems to be a galloping horse, and Rex Stewart, as the night advances, becomes progressively more cocky and springy as he takes his solos."

Ellington's personal physician and closest friend. According to Logan's widow, civil rights activist Marian Logan, the two men developed "a unique, incredible, unexplainable friendship." They saw each other or spoke by phone daily, even when Ellington was overseas. Often, he would call Logan from some distant point and half-seriously ask, "How am I today, Arthur?"[78]

The following year Ellington met another steady companion, a woman named Evie Ellis, a great beauty who worked at the Cotton Club. Ellington left Mildred Dixon and moved into Evie's place soon after they met. Meanwhile Ellington's sister, Ruth, now a student at Columbia, and Mercer, still in high school, moved to their own apartment. Duke and Evie lived together for the rest of his life. She was accepted as Ellington's common-law wife and often referred to herself as Mrs. Ellington. Even after Edna's death in 1966, Evie was convinced that Duke would someday marry her, but Ellington always

resisted. Evie's fierce protection of Duke from unwanted visitors or hangers-on—and her rage whenever she felt threatened by a rival for Ellington's affections—earned her the nickname Thunderbird.

Swing Arrives

As the thirties rolled on, the widespread economic depression, added to Ellington's personal depression after his mother's death, meant that gigs were increasingly scarce. Despite Mills's relatively successful efforts to secure engagements, Ellington just did not have the energy to follow through on them.

Then, in 1935, a new style of music swept America and posed the most serious challenge yet to Ellington's position in popular music. This was swing, a highly rhythmic big band sound. For thousands of young people swing became a way of

In 1938 Ellington left Mildred and moved in with Evie Ellis. Although they never married, the couple remained together until his death. They are pictured here in 1967.

Putting Niagara Falls to Shame

Gene Lees, in his essay "The Enigma: Duke Ellington," recalls his first sight of the Ellington band, in Niagara Falls, Ontario, Canada, during the band's glory years.

"I must have been ten or eleven. I was visiting my grandmother, and on a weekend summer evening I was out tooling around on my grandfather's bicycle . . . when I saw a crowd gathering in front of the arena on Lundy's Lane. I paused to consider this and heard music. So I [managed to] slip into the building through a rear exit. And there were these men, black, brown, and beige (as Duke put it in a suite), with their shining brass instruments, and a drummer with a great Oriental gong behind him (which immediately identifies him as Sonny Greer) and this suave man with a pencil mustache at the piano, collectively emitting a roar of music that put Niagara Falls to shame. . . . I must have stayed there all evening. No doubt my grandmother was frantic with worry. No doubt she raised hell when I got home. But I don't remember that. I remember only the music."

life. As John Edward Hasse noted, they "sought out radio broadcasts from remote locations, followed their favorite bands, auditioned the latest records, argued the merits of soloists and leaders, trekked off to famous dance halls, queued [lined] up to see bands perform on theater stages, and generally reveled in the music."[79]

Ironically, swing relied on a style pioneered years before by musicians like Ellington, though his music was different in several ways. Ellington liked long, complex melodies, while swing was built on short, repeated musical phrases called riffs. Ellington relied on the special talents of individual musicians; swing bands did not. And Ellington favored dense, complicated harmonies, while swing harmony was relatively simple.

The average listener found swing accessible and easy to understand, although die-hard fans and many musicians acknowledged that Ellington's music was more interesting.

By the late 1930s swing was the dominant form of popular music. The so-called King of Swing was Benny Goodman, a classically trained clarinetist. Other top bandleaders included Tommy and Jimmy Dorsey, Glenn Miller, Harry James, and Artie Shaw. Ellington gained little from this craze he had helped invent a decade earlier. It must have been painful for him to watch other bands rocket past him in popularity and financial reward. Still, Ellington remained philosophical, at least in public. He once remarked, "Jazz is music; swing is business."[80]

Ellington's band performs in a scene from the 1934 movie Murder at the Vanities. *The thirties were lucrative for the band—they appeared in several motion pictures, had a number of hit songs, and embarked on two successful European tours.*

Competition was fierce on all sides. By 1938 Count Basie's powerhouse band was rivaling Ellington as the top black orchestra. Though he disliked being lumped in with swing bands, Ellington was forced to take part in battles of the bands, in which rivals would try to outdo each other. He generally managed to prevail; at one such battle, called a Carnival of Swing, with twenty-five thousand people attending, Ellington's was the biggest hit among twenty orchestras.

Ellington managed to stay active in other ways. In 1938 he wrote the score for a new revue at the Cotton Club, his first in eight years. One song dropped from the revue, "I Let a Song Go Out of My Heart," became one of Ellington's biggest hits after he played it on the radio and was swamped with requests. It was also a good year for recording. Ellington recorded several classics, including "Prelude to a Kiss" and "Jeep's Blues," a wonderful small-band feature for Johnny Hodges. Radio was also lucrative. In addition to regular broadcasts, Ellington tunes were now being used as theme songs on thirty-seven radio programs—more than those of any other composer.

The band also continued to make movies, including two features, *Belle of the Nineties*, with Mae West, and *Murder at the Vanities*, in which a classical conductor shoots the band because they dared to jazz up one of Franz Liszt's Hungarian rhapsodies. A 1934 short subject, *Symphony in Black*, represented Ellington's longest single musical piece to date. The film was also the first time that a movie told a story through music only, instead of spoken dialogue. One of its performers was an unknown nineteen-year-old woman named Billie Holiday, who went on to become one of the most exquisite singers in jazz.

More Changes

For the first half of the thirties, Ellington's personnel had remained stable; several players had joined the band, but no one had permanently left since Bubber Miley in 1929. Late in 1934, however, trumpeter Freddie Jenkins contracted tuberculosis and was replaced by Rex Stewart. Soon after, Arthur Whetsol, who had been with the band since the beginning, succumbed to a brain tumor. Ellington also replaced bassist Wellman Braud with a young player, Billy Taylor. (This bassist was no relation to Dr. Billy Taylor, the well-known pianist, educator, and broadcaster).

Another change came when Ellington broke his long-standing relationship with Irving Mills. One day Ellington walked into Mills's office, asked to see the account books, then left without a word. Shortly afterwards Ellington informed Mills that he wanted to end their partnership.

Ellington had apparently suspected for some time that Mills was taking advantage of him. The final straw was the discovery that Mills had cheated on Ellington's mother's funeral. Ellington had asked Mills to buy an expensive casket, but Mills had bought a cheap one and manipulated the accounts. Ellington had also been under pressure from black leaders to break with Mills. They felt that Mills, by unfairly using himself as Ellington's lyricist, was taking opportunities that should have gone to blacks. An influential Afro-American newspaper, the Pittsburgh *Courier*, wrote, "No Negro writer has written the lyrics for any of Duke Ellington's melodies since he has been under the Mills banner. What's the matter, Duke? House rules?"[81]

On the other hand, Ellington may simply have felt he had learned enough to go on without Mills. In any event, in 1939 he signed with the powerful William Morris Agency. Ellington's business was now handled by a smart, aggressive young man, Cress Courtney, who would work with Ellington for years. Born wheeler-dealers, Courtney and Ellington instantly understood each other. The young manager recalled that at one of their first meetings he tried to persuade Ellington to close his shows with a lively tune, instead of the usual slow number. Courtney recalled, "And after I got through talking with him, he said to me, 'That's a beautiful tie.' And I said, 'That's the deal, huh?' And he said, 'Yeah.' And I said, 'OK, Here's your tie. Now play your goddamn fast music.'"[83]

Before the split Irving Mills had arranged a return European tour for Ellington. When the band arrived in France in March 1939, *downbeat* magazine reported that "hundreds of jitterbugs stomped and shouted at the dock."[83] The band was as warmly received as it had been on the first tour. Rex Stewart recalled, "Fans and musicians . . . all greeted us with such absolute adoration and genuine joy that for the first time in my life I had the feeling of being accepted as an artist, a gentleman and a member of the human race."[84]

Virtually all performances on this tour were in concert halls, not vaudeville theaters or dance halls. Concerts in Paris, Brussels, the Hague, Utrecht, and Amsterdam were sold out. In Antwerp the producers printed a twelve-page program as a mark of respect for Ellington's music. The sight of impending war was everywhere, however; Ellington recalled seeing machine-gun posts as the band passed

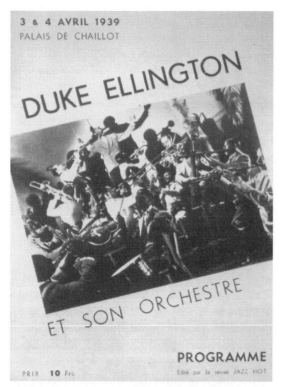

The program cover for a 1939 performance in Paris. The band's second European tour was a huge success—they once again delighted audiences and played to sold-out concert halls across Europe.

through Holland. En route to Denmark and Sweden, the group had to travel through Germany and was stranded for six scary hours in the Hamburg station among swarms of openly hostile Nazi soldiers.

But the fans and critics in Scandinavia were ecstatic. One newspaper reported, "The platforms of the railway stations, all along the route, were filled with people hoping to get a glimpse of the Duke. He and his famous orchestra practically played all the way to Stockholm."[85] On April 29, Duke's fortieth birthday, he was awakened in his Stockholm hotel by a sixteen-piece band, and flowers arrived all day long.

During a concert that evening the audience sang a birthday song in Swedish, and ten little girls dressed in white sang "Happy Birthday" in English. (One of the girls was Alice Babs, who years later would be an important soloist in Ellington's sacred concerts.) In return, Ellington offered a new piece, "Serenade to Sweden," which was broadcast across the country. As he had the first time, Ellington loved the attention and the relative lack of racism. He once remarked:

> Europe is a very different world from [America]. You can go anywhere and talk to anybody and do anything you like. It's hard to believe. When you've eaten hot dogs all your life and you're suddenly offered caviar, it's hard to believe it's true.[86]

Unfortunately the threat of war forced the band to cut its tour short, and in early May they sailed home. Ellington would not visit Europe again until 1948. Instead, he would ride out the war years at home.

7 The War Years

The memory of things gone is important to a jazz musician. Things like folks singing in the moonlight in the backyard, or a hot night, or something someone said long ago.

—Duke Ellington

Throughout the 1940s Ellington was hitting his stride. He won poll after poll as America's top black bandleader. He turned out a long string of hit records.

And his more serious compositions also got genuine attention. A major reason for this creative surge was the arrival of a brilliant young man from Pittsburgh named Billy Strayhorn.

Strayhorn had been trained as a classical pianist and composer, but as a high school student he heard the Ellington band perform and was hooked. Just before the band's second European trip in 1939, Strayhorn, then twenty-three, worked up the courage to introduce himself backstage

Hired as Ellington's lyricist in 1939, Billy Strayhorn quickly proved himself a talented composer as well. The pair is pictured here with actor Danny Kaye (right) in 1945.

after a show in Newark, New Jersey. He played some pieces for his hero. Ellington was impressed by Strayhorn's gift for words and told him to come to New York and be his lyricist.

Strayhorn left for New York immediately, moving in with Ruth and Mercer while the band was in Europe. Within months he had contributed an arrangement and an original piece for a recording session, displaying a talent for much more than lyric writing. By the end of the year he was listed as co-composer on five pieces. Strayhorn showed an immediate

rapport for Ellington's unusual, sometimes difficult music. He once remarked, "His first, last and only formal instruction for me was embodied in one word: observe. I did just that, and came to know one of the most fascinating and original minds in American music."[87]

In many ways, however, the two men were opposites. Ellington was tall, imposing, and sleekly handsome; Strayhorn was short and slight, with thick glasses and a boyish face. Ellington lived his life theatrically, charming and manipulating as he went; Strayhorn was shy and avoided the

"In the Tradition of Bach and Haydn"

In this passage from a 1943 New York Times Magazine *article reprinted in Mark Tucker's* Duke Ellington Reader, *writer Howard Taubman comments on Ellington's similarities to the great classical composers.*

"Ellington's music and band must be discussed as a unit, for they have been made for each other during the past twenty years. Though it may shock the idolaters [worshipers] of the masters, it is fair to say that Ellington is a composer in the tradition of Bach and Haydn. The eighteenth-century masters wrote most of their music for specific occasions, for performances by themselves and ensembles under their leadership and often under pressure of a deadline. That's the way Ellington works. His public wants new pieces. Ellington turns them out at the last minute. He writes them only with his own band in mind.

Even the copying out of the parts of a new Ellington composition is reminiscent of the way Bach is supposed to have worked. Bach's sons copied out parts even as their father composed. Members of Duke's band sat up with him through an all-night session, as he wrote a fairly long new piece, and extracted the parts for the individual players as fast as Duke set down the music on the master score. Several times, when Duke's muse seemed to be slowing up, his copyists jogged him: 'C'mon, Duke,' they said, 'you're holding us up.' And Ellington worked a little faster."

spotlight. Ellington was a notorious womanizer who rarely spent long with a lover; Strayhorn, who was homosexual, happily stayed with one partner for many years.

Everybody loved young Strayhorn's sweet nature. The band nicknamed him Strays and Swee'Pea, the latter in honor of a lovable baby adopted by Popeye in the comic strip, and informally adopted him. Ellington became a father figure to Strayhorn, who was sixteen years younger and from a troubled family; in return, Strays gave Duke utter devotion. Strayhorn also gave Ellington free rein to control the relationship. Singer Lena Horne, a close friend of both, once remarked:

> Duke was a father figure, without a doubt, and certainly a better one than Billy's own father. . . . The problem is, Duke treated Billy exactly like he treated women, with all that old-fashioned chauvinism. Very loving and very protective, but controlling, very destructive.[88]

Composing

Strayhorn's training in composition and arranging let Ellington do away with his informal, unusual methods of composing. Ellington used the whole band as if it were one instrument; in fact, he often remarked that his true instrument was not the piano but the entire orchestra. His usual method was to slowly work out a piece by rehearsing it with the band a few bars at a time, accepting criticism and suggestions as he went. Juan Tizol would write down a rough score of the emerging piece for Ellington to polish. Now Ellington could let Strays work out the technical details.

The leader continued, however, to borrow and embellish ideas that had been supplied by other players. Some of the musicians resented this; Johnny Hodges, for instance, would shoot Ellington a dirty look and demand a raise when he heard a musical phrase he had suggested. Sometimes Hodges even turned to Ellington on the bandstand and mimed the counting of money while a borrowed piece was being played. Helen Dance, a critic and a friend of Ellington's, once remarked, "Every time Duke would take a few notes that were Johnny's, Johnny would clear his throat and give him one of his looks out of the side of his eye, and Duke knew that Johnny figured this was a hundred dollars."[89]

Ellington also continued his habit of composing anytime, anywhere: in trains on the backs of envelopes, in late-night buses with someone holding up matches so he could see, in the recording studio with sheet music propped up on the window of the booth—even in the bathtub. One friend recalled finding Ellington soaking in a hotel tub with a stack of manuscript paper, a container of chocolate ice cream, a glass of scotch and milk, and Jonesy, his valet, close at hand. (Jonesy's job was to maintain an even temperature in the tub.) When Ellington wrote down something he wanted to hear, he sang it to Strayhorn, who was in the bedroom next door. Strayhorn played the idea on an upright piano; Duke listened, then nodded his head and wrote some more.

Some Join, Some Leave

Several key players joined the band during this time. In the fall of 1939 Ellington

Bassist Jimmy Blanton signed on with Ellington's band in 1939, and in a short time revolutionized the role of the bass player in jazz music.

hired a second bass player, whose short career revolutionized the bass's role in jazz. Jimmy Blanton did not play in the old-fashioned slap-bass style, in which the bass does little more than keep time. Instead, he played as if the bass was capable of soloing as melodically as any instrument. Ellington's other bassist, Billy Taylor, continued with the band until January 1940 when, according to legend, he walked offstage and said, "I'm not going to stand up here next to that young boy playing all that bass and be embarrassed."[90]

Another important addition was tenor saxophonist Ben Webster. Webster had a romantic, emotional sound and although he became the band's fifth saxophonist, he was its first full-time tenor player. Herb Jeffries, a singer with a flexible voice that ranged from light baritone to falsetto, was added to handle vocals with Ivie Anderson. And there was Mercer Ellington, who had formed his own band, with limited success, and had tried his hand at other areas of music. In 1940 he finally bowed to the inevitable and joined the Ellington band's trumpet section.

But in 1940 the band suffered a major loss, when Benny Goodman wooed trumpet star Cootie Williams away. Williams was an eleven-year veteran of the band, and his departure was stunning. As James Lincoln Collier put it, "In the jazz world it was a little as if the Pope had converted to Buddhism."[91] One bandleader even wrote a piece called "When Cootie Left the Duke." It was not a sudden move, however. "I didn't just jump up and leave—I wouldn't do that," Williams said. "Duke knew about it, and helped set everything up. He got me more money, and I told him I'd be back in one year's time."[92] During Williams's absence he was replaced by Ray Nance, whose varied talents—trumpet, violin, vocals, and dancing—earned him the nickname Floorshow.

More losses followed. Jimmy Blanton, who had contracted tuberculosis, was forced to leave in November 1941; he died seven months later. Next came the departures of Herb Jeffries and Ivie Anderson. Jeffries was replaced by a series of male singers, including the blind baritone Al Hibbler. Anderson was replaced by a string of female vocalists, including unrelated Marie Ellington, a deep-voiced beauty who later married Nat "King" Cole.

Wartime conditions were part of the reason the band lost two more key players in the summer of 1942. Gasoline and tires were rationed, so travel by car or bus had become impossible; the band had also lost its special rail cars. It was forced to use public rail cars so crowded that the musicians often had to sit in the aisles. Barney Bigard and Juan Tizol, both eager to settle down with their new wives, decided to leave the road.

The Classic Recordings

The early 1940s Ellington band represented, for many fans, the golden age. As writer and critic Raymond Horricks put it, that band had "a lust for life; it hit harder musically, bit deeper emotionally, and swung more animatedly . . . than any Ellington band that preceded it."[93] In part this was because the players had an average of eight to ten years with Ellington— much longer than usual for jazz musicians. Ellington was able to keep these players with him partly by offering constant inspiration and challenge; as Ben Webster put it, "Duke is a great guy to work for. He understands musicians better than any other leader."[94] The high salaries he paid did not hurt; when asked by a British interviewer what was needed to keep a band together, Ellington once replied, "Well, you've got to have a gimmick. The gimmick I use is—I give them money."[95]

The recordings produced during this period are among Ellington's finest, and many of Ellington's most famous pieces date from this time, including "Cotton Tail," "Never No Lament," "Jack the Bear," "I Got It Bad," "Ko-Ko," "Caravan," com-

Ellington's band suffered the loss of a number of members in the forties, including eleven-year veteran Cootie Williams (center). The talented trumpeter left to join Benny Goodman's band.

posed by Juan Tizol, and the Strayhorn composition that became Ellington's signature tune, "Take the A Train." Besides being popular hits, these compositions were brilliantly compact masterpieces of writing. Gunther Schuller, a distinguished composer and Ellington scholar, observed that they "let in a gust of spontaneity, of freshness, of flexibility . . . which offered a whole new way of integrating composition and improvisation."[96]

Besides strong playing and composition, the early 1940s records had other factors working in their favor. The technical quality was excellent. The recording contract Ellington signed with Victor had two unusual clauses: one ensured that no other black big band could record for Victor's full-priced label as long as Ellington was on it, and the other allowed Ellington to choose his own material.

Unfortunately this period of creativity for Ellington soon came to an end, primarily because of wartime. Shellac for records became scarce, and so many fans and musicians were drafted that there were fall-offs in record sales and the number of available musicians. Then, in 1942, a recording ban was imposed by the musicians' union; except for a few radio transcriptions, no instrumental music could be recorded. This was good for singers but not for instrumentalists, and for a few years Ellington only occasionally made recordings. However the ban did not stop him from becoming one of the first black composers to form his own publishing firm. By taking complete control of his music and royalties in this way, Ellington became wealthy; he also became a pioneer in increasing the power and independence enjoyed by Afro-American artists.

Jump for Joy

In 1941 Ellington, with writer Sid Kuller and lyricist Paul Webster, created an all-black musical, *Jump for Joy*, that was probably the first big-time show to portray Afro-Americans in nonstereotyped ways.

"Some Kind of Signal"

Sometimes, John Edward Hasse points out in Beyond Category, *the Ellington orchestra actually composed while in different rooms of a hotel.*

"The band seemed to be all on the same floor of the hotel . . . and the sound of Strays at the keyboard was like some kind of signal. Pretty soon you'd hear Ben Webster playing a line, then Ray Nance would start tooting from somewhere down the hall. Sonny Greer would come in with his sticks, and the music would start to form . . . and about four or five choruses later, two more songs for the show were finished."

A publicity photo for Jump for Joy, *an all-black musical with a strong antiracist message. Ellington cocreated the musical, which despite excellent reviews folded after only eleven weeks.*

The show had a strong antiracist message. As one of its cast members put it, "Everything, every setting, every note of music, every lyric, meant something."[97]

Its songs, including "Uncle Tom's Cabin Is a Drive-In Now" and "I've Got a Passport from Georgia and I'm Sailing for the U.S.A.," were strong and, at the time, extremely bold statements. *Jump for Joy* received rave reviews but folded after only eleven weeks, doomed by uneven quality and competition from other popular musicals. Its serious theme may also have hurt it at a time when the public craved simple entertainment. Nonetheless, Ellington always referred to it as "the hippest thing we ever did."

A few years later another major Ellington performance took place: his debut at Carnegie Hall. This historic 1943 concert was the first opportunity ever for a black composer to present an evening of original music at New York's, and America's, most prestigious concert hall. Ellington recalled that he was so busy beforehand that it was the only time he did not suffer from pre-performance stage fright. "I just didn't have time," he said. "I couldn't afford the luxury of being scared."[98]

Black, Brown, and Beige

The high point of the three-hour concert was the premiere of an ambitious forty-four-minute suite Ellington had been working on since 1930. *Black, Brown, and Beige: A Tone Parallel to the History of the Negro in America* outlined a spectrum of Afro-American life, including such aspects as work, church, emancipation, the blues, and the progress of civil rights. Despite its serious themes, *Black, Brown, and Beige* is overall a powerful statement of pride and hope.

Critical reaction to *Black, Brown, and Beige* was mixed; several commentators felt that portions were not up to Ellington's usual standards. This was a bitter disappointment to the composer, and the negative reaction may have kept him from performing the piece more extensively. Except for two concerts held shortly after the Carnegie event, Ellington never performed the piece in its entirety again.

Despite the negative reaction, Carnegie was a major turning point for Ellington. After spending twenty years as a top bandleader, after making more than seven hundred recordings and selling nearly twenty million records, after creating a kind of music no one had ever heard before, and after triumphing in Europe's concert halls, Ellington had finally performed in his own country's foremost hall—not a dance palace or a nightclub, but a *concert hall*. Ellington performed six more Carnegie concerts, each featuring extended new pieces, but the first one was the most important. "This event and the scope of 'Black, Brown and Beige' altered [Ellington's] reputation and patterns of composing and performing," John Edward Hasse noted. "In addition to his other mantles [cloaks], from now on, he would wear that of concert artist."[99]

The Rest of the War

Although musicians in general suffered during World War II, Ellington generally prospered. Financially the war years were good for Ellington. Tunes like "Don't Get Around Much Anymore," "Do Nothin' till You Hear from Me," and "I'm Beginning to See the Light" were jukebox hits. Several of his musicians, including Mercer, were drafted into the military, but the leader himself was spared. Ellington had planned to take an army physical in early 1943; a month before his appointment, however, a decision was made not to draft men over thirty-eight. Instead, Ellington helped the war effort by playing benefits, and the band performed frequently on military bases.

He and his band continued to appear in movies, including the all-black musical *Cabin in the Sky* with Louis Armstrong and Lena Horne. Orson Welles, the brilliant director of *Citizen Kane*, hired Ellington for a project called *It's All True*, which was never finished. Welles once remarked that Ellington was the only genius besides himself he had ever met. The recording ban was still in effect, but the orchestra made nearly one hundred half-hour recorded programs for broadcast to the armed forces. The band also did about fifty hour-long network radio shows, *Your Saturday*

Flowing and Flowing

Ellington's ability to write anywhere—on trains, in recording studios, on buses, in hotel rooms—was remarkable, as John Edward Hasse notes in Beyond Category.

"A writer might do his best work only at a favorite desk, a sculptor at her own studio, a composer at a special piano. That Ellington could turn out dozens, even hundreds, of inspired compositions while criss-crossing the nation, often in the musical equivalent of a politician's whistle-stop tour, is astounding. It took an individual of enormous purpose, flexibility, and calm to enable his creative juices to flow and flow and flow."

Ellington plays for servicemen in Hartford, Connecticut, in 1942. Too old to be drafted, Ellington contributed to the war effort by playing benefits and performing on military bases.

Date with the Duke, sponsored by the Treasury Department to help sell war bonds.

The war and the years brought further personnel changes. Ben Webster, Ray Nance, and Rex Stewart all left to form their own bands. Tricky Sam Nanton had a stroke and was forced to retire. And one night Otto Hardwick walked offstage, allegedly in a dispute with Ellington over a woman, and never again played professionally. But the group gained some important new members. Clarinetist Jimmy Hamilton joined in 1943 and stayed for twenty-five years. Another fine clarinet player, Russell Procope, came on board in 1946 and stayed until Ellington's death in 1974. And Ellington added a new trumpet star, high-note specialist Cat Anderson. *Variety* magazine once wrote of Anderson, "One note higher and only a dog could hear him."[100]

During these years Ellington kept up a breakneck schedule, largely because he needed to meet a huge payroll. By 1944 he had twenty-nine people on salary—including musicians, copyists, valets, and a barber. Bringing a barber on tour was not a luxury. The band's odd schedule meant that its members could rarely visit barbershops at normal times, and a sharp appearance was always an important part of the Ellington mystique. Salaries were always high—Ellington's wages were generally as good as or better than any bandleader's. Everyone was paid in cash, and the band's road managers often carried guns to protect the payroll. Ellington also traveled with a gun—an antique revolver he called Sweetie Mae.

Like most Americans, Ellington had to deal with deprivation and loss during the war, though in general he prevailed as he had done during the depression. Many fans feel that his writing and the band's playing were never stronger. But the war years also created an instability in the band's ranks from which it never recovered.

8 Hard Times

Why should I knock myself out in an argument about fifteen dollars when in the same time I can probably write a fifteen-hundred-dollar song?

—Duke Ellington

In the early 1950s the big band era was ending. The cost of maintaining a huge orchestra was too high for virtually everyone; famous bandleaders like Goodman, Basie, and the Dorsey brothers were forced to tour with groups of only six or eight performers. Audiences preferred to listen to individual singers, such as Frank Sinatra and Doris Day, who had originally risen to fame with big bands. For dancing, younger audiences preferred the newer styles of rhythm and blues or rock and roll.

At the same time, a new style of jazz called bebop was taking over. Pioneered by Miles Davis, Dizzy Gillespie, Charlie "Bird" Parker, and others, it was more abstract than dance-oriented swing and featured

The forties ushered in a new fast-paced, wildly improvised style of jazz called bebop, popularized by such performers as saxophonist Charlie "Bird" Parker (center) and trumpeter Miles Davis (right).

"Kissy-Pink Moustaches"

In this passage from a 1952 interview, reprinted in Peter Gammond's Duke Ellington: His Life and Music, *Ellington muses on the role his musicians played in his creativity.*

"Right now I think I've got a helluva great band, and so naturally I think we've got a great period ahead of us. Stimulating soloists have always made me want to write, and we certainly have a lot of them in our band today. It's when I have men like these to write for that I get a germ of an idea and these germs are different. They are the ones with pink wings and violet blue polka dots and kissy-pink moustaches and golden spats and multicolored tails. They're the germs of the ideas that I'm going to put into music."

angular melodies, long improvisations, and fast tempos. Several bebop pioneers played briefly with Ellington. The brilliant saxophonist Charlie Parker wanted to join the band but demanded $500 a week; Ellington reportedly replied, "Bird, for that kind of dough I'd work for you."

All this change meant tough times for Ellington. He was still a famous and honored figure. In 1952, for instance, *downbeat* magazine devoted an entire issue to his twenty-fifth anniversary in music. But beboppers, not Ellington, were now the cutting edge artists. His music seemed to many to be a shadow of its former glory. One soured critic wrote, "Isn't it about time the Ellington orchestra was disbanded before what's left of a great reputation is completely dragged in the muck?"[101]

Recording dates began to dry up. After an unsuccessful attempt to start his own label, Ellington signed with Columbia in 1948, for whom he recorded off and on. But another union strike, which banned all instrumental recordings for a

year, forced him to stop only four months into the new contract. When the ban was lifted, Columbia was in no hurry to record Ellington because by then solo vocalists—never his strong suit—were in vogue.

Constant touring and Ellington's determination kept the band alive. The orchestra was no longer making a profit, but Ellington financed it through his song royalties. At an age and in a financial position when many people would have retired, he could not let the band go. The orchestra was his life. As he often put it, "What would I retire *to*?"

Despite these problems the band had several high points. It made more European tours, including one in 1950 that saw seventy-four concerts in seventy-seven days. The band continued to do well in annual popularity polls. Ellington's first long-playing record was released in 1950. The orchestra was featured in three short movies. And some excellent music came out of this period, notably a fourteen-minute work called "Harlem Air Shaft"

Admiring crowds welcome Ellington (waving hat) as his band arrives in Milan, Italy, during their 1950 European tour. The band performed seventy-four concerts during the hectic seventy-seven-day tour.

commissioned by the NBC Symphony Orchestra and premiered at the Metropolitan Opera House in New York City.

"The Skin Disease"

By now the band played mostly grueling one-nighters under rough conditions. Private rail cars were a long-gone luxury, and the band traveled mainly by bus, although Ellington usually traveled by car with Harry Carney, and racism was still common. Road manager Al Celley, who was white, often had to go into a restaurant to ask if the rest of the band could come in.

In 1951 the NAACP threatened to picket an Ellington concert in Richmond, Virginia, because the audience would be segregated. Ellington angrily canceled the gig and complained that the lost opportunity hurt all the members of his band. A reporter claimed that Ellington told him

that black people "ain't ready" to fight segregation, and this comment created a huge uproar in the black press. Ellington later denied having made the statement. He defended his upholding of civil rights, said the NAACP should not picket black artists, and called for a major nationwide movement to end racism.

The question of Ellington's attitude toward racism—which he called "the skin disease"—was an old one. Since the 1930s Ellington had been criticized because he refused to take a militant stand. He felt that the best way he could help was through music and by setting a positive example, but some people felt it was not enough. Back in 1935 critic John Hammond, who was white but fought passionately for black causes, had accused Ellington of being insensitive to race issues and of paying too much attention to European-style composition. Writer Enzo Archetti had replied, "Fortunately, Ellington is too great an artist and too important a creator to be influenced by such reactions."[102]

Ellington seemed to take both criticism and racism in stride. Until his death he remained outwardly calm about the fact that, as a black man, he could not eat in most restaurants or sleep in most hotels in the United States. He said he simply could not be bothered—he had more pressing matters on his mind. As he once remarked, "I took the energy it takes to pout and wrote some blues."[103]

Besides, Ellington felt, he had made his own inroads against racism. Back in the 1930s his orchestra had broken a number of barriers: first black band to make an extended engagement at a downtown Dallas club, first to play a white Austin hotel, first to perform at the University of Texas, first to play to a large white audience in Memphis. Even then he had disdained the term *jazz*, preferring to call his music "Negro music" or "the music of my people." And the music itself had always been about Afro-American pride, hope, joy, and strength. Ellington was ashamed of nothing.

Still a Hit with the Ladies

Ellington's reputation as a womanizer had been well established when he was a teenager, and it continued full speed even as he became older and even when times were tough for him. He simply could not stop himself from flirting with pretty women, and they responded in kind more often than not. As Sonny Greer put it, "Duke drew people to him like flies to sugar."[104]

On one occasion his reputation made him the victim of a hoax while on the road in Chicago. A refined-sounding con man posing as Ellington began phoning prominent married women to ask for "a quiet date." For five nights in a row Ellington came back to his hotel to find passionate

Ellington surrounded by Parisian women in 1939. Despite his common-law marriage to Evie Ellis, Ellington continued to live up to his reputation as a womanizer.

messages waiting for him from the wives of attorneys, physicians, and the like. When word of the hoax leaked to the press, Ellington told a reporter, probably with a twinkle in his eye, "Being a married man, you can imagine just how embarrassing it was."[105]

There are many stories about Ellington and women. His usual introduction to the song "Satin Doll" was, "Ladies and gentlemen, the next song is dedicated to the most beautiful lady here. We will not point her out because we do not want her to feel conspicuous. We will just let her sit there and continue to feel guilty."[106]

On one occasion in San Francisco, he was late for a club date. The band had already been onstage for some time, and the crowd was grumbling and visibly angered. When Ellington finally made it onstage, there were even a few boos from the audience. Ellington sat down at the piano, turned to the audience with his most charming smile, and said, "Ladies and Gentlemen. . . . If you had seen her, you would understand." From that moment on, the audience was in the palm of his hand.

All through the years of his womanizing, Ellington continued to live with Evie Ellis when he was in New York. They were generally recognized as man and wife, and she continued to refer to herself as Mrs. Ellington. But their relationship gradually turned into a love-hate affair. Ellington took her presence for granted, assuming she would always be there for him. She, meanwhile, expected to be taken care of lavishly. She often knew about Ellington's outside affairs and periodically flew into rages about them, but always somehow managed to forgive him. They never had children, and Evie instead lavished attention on Davy, her poodle.

On one occasion Evie unexpectedly flew to Tokyo to visit Ellington. She found him in the company of another woman. Ellington forcefully told Evie that he would not let her embarrass him in any way and that she should fly home immedi-

Drug and Alcohol Abuse by Band Members

Ellington turned a blind eye toward the abuse of drugs and alcohol by band members. In his memoir, Duke Ellington in Person, *Mercer Ellington writes of this tolerance.*

"Pop's attitude toward drugs was governed by the fact that the musician was an artist, and he recognized that artists were given to strange ways of living. He never admonished anyone for anything he did that was wrong in the eyes of society. If you did something that was a direct affront [offense] to him, he had a way of getting the point across to you that he was angry. But he wasn't bothered so much by the impact of wrongdoing on the world because basically what he wanted to hear was the music, and he believed the people he had were the ones to play it."

Johnny Hodges (pictured with Ellington), Sonny Greer, and Lawrence Brown left the band in 1951 to form their own band. Ellington felt saddened and betrayed by the departure of these three longtime members.

ately. She did and then hid out at Mercer's apartment so that Ellington could not contact her. When Ellington did return, he was loaded down with expensive presents and succeeded in making up with her. "Theirs was a strange relationship," Mercer Ellington wrote in his memoirs, "but the only way I can really gauge its depth is by the proportion of his life he spent with her and by the fact that he never considered leaving her for any reason, although he had to spend a great amount of time away from her."[107]

The Bottom

Throughout this period the band suffered several more key losses. In 1949 guitarist Fred Guy, a band member since the days of the Club Kentucky, left and was not replaced. Sonny Greer, a founding member,

had alcohol-related health problems, and Ellington had to hire a backup drummer to tour with the band. Then, in 1951, three longtime band members—Greer, trombonist Lawrence Brown, and Johnny Hodges—announced that they had secretly arranged to form a new band with Hodges as the leader.

Each of these players was important, and together they had seventy years of experience with the orchestra. But Hodges was most closely linked with the Ellington sound. It is unclear exactly why he left, but money probably played a big role; Hodges never felt his salary was enough to compensate for his contributions. Hodges also liked the small-combo format and was uncomfortable with Ellington's classically oriented pieces. Furthermore, like many other musicians, Hodges had a large ego and liked the idea of leading a band. Still, the announcement came as a shock. As John Edward Hasse put it, "It was a stunning blow, the greatest professional crisis Ellington had ever faced."[108]

Ellington's reaction to the press ranged from jaunty to somber. To one reporter he remarked, "I'm a young bandleader starting out all over again."[109] To another he said, "There is no such thing as a 'replacement' in my band. A new musician means for us a new sound and the creation of new music, which he, and he alone, can properly express."[110] Privately, he must have been angry and sad. Loyalty was always important to him, and when he felt betrayed he was hurt.

Ellington compensated by recruiting several excellent new players: trombonist Britt Woodman, tenor saxophonist Paul Gonsalves, and trumpeters Willie Cook and Clark Terry. He also replaced Hodges, Brown, and Greer with three powerful players. He brought Juan Tizol back from semi-retirement, put saxophonist Willie Smith in Hodges's place, and recruited Louis Bellson to be the band's drummer. Bellson, the first white musician to be a regular member of the Ellington band, was only twenty-five at the time, but had done fiery work with Benny Goodman and Tommy Dorsey. Although he did not stay long with Ellington—he left to marry singer Pearl Bailey and work with her band—Bellson provided much-needed voltage.

Television had taken over the entertainment scene, sweeping the country wildly. In 1950, 9 percent of American households had television sets, but by 1960 the figure was up to 87 percent. Ellington saw that television was the wave of the future. In 1955 he wrote, "The future of big band existence in the entertainment industry, I firmly believe, is closely associated with television."[111] The band made short films for television, but Ellington never got a solid audience, while singers like Dinah Shore and Nat "King" Cole hosted popular shows.

Long-playing records (LPs) gave Ellington a chance to explore extended works and themes, and their rise should have been a boost. But he mistakenly signed with Capitol, a label better at selling than at maintaining quality. Capitol teamed Ellington with a less-than-brilliant producer who had the band recording mambos, tangos, and other faddish styles. One good LP did emerge from this period, however: a recording session with only piano, bass, and drums called *Duke Plays Ellington*, also titled *Piano Reflections*.

Ellington's composing was also at a low ebb. Between 1951 and 1956 he premiered only one big new piece, "Night Creature." During this period the band made no movies and took no overseas trips. In the summer of 1955 Ellington was forced to take a gig accompanying a water show with ice skaters. Third on the bill, he ran the orchestra through a medley of hits, then stood by as another conductor took over. Adding insult to injury, Ellington was forced to lay off four players during this demeaning job because they did not belong to the local union.

But Ellington's fortunes were about to change. The following summer, at the Newport Jazz Festival in the posh seaside town of Newport, Rhode Island, Ellington made history.

"Don't Be Rude to the Artists!"

The stakes were high when Ellington was asked to play the festival's closing concert.

Johnny Hodges had recently rejoined, along with Cootie Williams, Juan Tizol, and Lawrence Brown. Ellington was also going to be the subject of an upcoming *Time* magazine cover story. He knew that his fans were waiting to see if the band could deliver. By the time Ellington took the stage, it was nearly midnight, and many in the audience had already left.

The band opened with *Newport Festival Suite*—not an outstanding piece—but then launched into its second number.

This was *Diminuendo and Crescendo in Blue*, a composition in two parts that dated from 1937. Ellington instructed tenor player Paul Gonsalves to come down front and play an improvised, up-tempo blues piece between the halves. As Gonsalves

"Like Rain on the Roof"

In his 1944 New Yorker *profile, reprinted in Mark Tucker's* Duke Ellington Reader, *writer Richard O. Boyer comments on the remarkable poise the bandleader maintained.*

"There are times when Duke Ellington exudes such calm contentment that a colleague, under the influence of the benign radiation, once murmured drowsily, 'Duke make me sleepy, like rain on the roof.' His nerves and laughter are so loose and easy that members of his jazz band believe that they got that way because of his physical makeup rather than because of the quality of his spirit. 'His pulse is so low he can't get excited,' they explain. . . . Only something in the flow of the blood, they are sure, could explain a calm that has survived twenty-three years in the band business—years in which Duke and his seventeen-piece band have again and again clattered on tour from one end of the country to the other. Duke believes that his calm is an acquired characteristic, attained through practice, but whether acquired or inborn, it is his monumental placidity [calmness], which is only occasionally shattered, that enables Duke to compose much of his music in an atmosphere of strident confusion. Most composers, along with their souls and their grand pianos, regard composition as a private activity. Often, when Duke is working out the details of a composition of an arrangement, the sixteen other members of his band not only are present but may even participate, and the occasion sometimes sounds like a political convention, sometimes like a zoo at feeding time."

came to center stage, the audience was enthusiastic but restrained. But then Gonsalves launched into a blazing solo, and the crowd started going wild.

By Gonsalves's sixth chorus the audience was clapping and shouting. Duke let Gonsalves play on, more and more passionately, and the crowd got wilder. Ellington knew something special was happening, and the showman in him was not about to stop it; on the recording made of that evening, Ellington's shouts of encouragement can be clearly heard. Then one woman started dancing, and Clark Terry recalled, "that really . . . fired Duke up and he fired us up. . . . The people were screamin' and hollerin' at her."[112]

Couples began dancing everywhere. People climbed on chairs. Fans rushed the stage as Gonsalves, his eyes squeezed shut, played chorus after chorus. Concert organizer George Wein, worried about a riot, shouted to Ellington to stop, which only annoyed the bandleader. Sensing he was making history, Ellington shook his finger at Wein and yelled, "Don't be rude to the artists!" Finally, after Gonsalves had played twenty-seven choruses in six minutes, Ellington gave a signal, and the band jumped into the second part of the written piece. When the band finally left the stage, after four more numbers, reporters rushed to find telephones so they could relay the news.

Six minutes of the blues had put Duke back on top. The *Time* story later that summer was a lucky coincidence that added to the excitement. After years of neglect, fans and critics suddenly began clamoring for more of Ellington. After surviving the hardest decade of his career, a single event launched him on another winning streak. As Whitney Balliett put it:

At the 1956 Newport Jazz Festival, Paul Gonsalves belted out a six-minute blues solo on the tenor sax that electrified the audience, and helped put Ellington back in the public eye. He is pictured during a 1971 performance in Russia.

A perverse, canny, exhilarating showbiz stunt of the kind Ellington generally abhorred [hated] gave him enough momentum to carry him through the rest of his life. He once said, his face straight and his tie tied, "I was born in 1956 at the Newport festival." Most of us, flat-footed and earnest, would have said reborn.[113]

9 Honors at Home and Abroad

Jazz is like the automobile and airplane. It is modern and it is American. . . . Jazz is the freedom to play anything, whether it has been done before or not. It gives you freedom.

—Duke Ellington

Much of the band's newfound strength was due to new musicians who used the orchestra as a training ground; Clark Terry called the band the University of Ellingtonia because so many young players came of age in it. But legendary old-timers like Hodges, Williams, Tizol, and Brown also added to the band's muscle. For these returnees, life outside the Ellington fold had proved unsatisfactory. As Ruth Ellington once remarked, "I've heard the band members say, 'When you leave Duke Ellington, there's no place else to go.'"[114]

It now cost Ellington over a million dollars a year just to keep his show on the road, but there was no shortage of work. After a live-at-Newport record became Ellington's biggest LP ever, Columbia was eager to record him. He was teamed with a sensitive producer, Irving Townsend, and they worked nonstop: between 1956 and 1962 Ellington recorded over twenty LPs' worth of material—an average of one every three and a half months! Ellington

and Strayhorn were writing or arranging a new piece about once a week. Strayhorn once said, "Even the unscheduled work is behind schedule."[115] In addition to the commercial recordings, Ellington privately recorded over three hundred pieces that were never released to the public.

The successful collaboration between Ellington and Strayhorn produced an astonishing number of new pieces—about one a week.

One major composition from this period was *A Drum Is a Woman*, about the mythical Madame Zajj, who travels from the Caribbean to New Orleans, New York, and the moon. Another, *Such Sweet Thunder*, was based on themes from Shakespeare. A third, *Suite Thursday*, is based on John Steinbeck's novel *Sweet Thursday*. Still other projects were adaptations of two classical works, *The Nutcracker* and *Peer Gynt*. Ellington also recorded two excellent albums highlighting his piano playing—*Piano in the Foreground* and *Money Jungle*—and made a string of delightful collaborations with such varied artists as Ella Fitzgerald, Rosemary Clooney, Coleman Hawkins, Frank Sinatra, Louis Armstrong, and John Coltrane. Not all of Ellington's recordings in the 1960s were as artistically successful; during a tenure at the Reprise label, he recorded some inferior material, including tunes from *Mary Poppins* and *Hello, Dolly!*

Ellington also did occasional film work. For the first time in twenty-five years, he was invited in 1959 to create the sound track for a film: *Anatomy of a Murder*, a thriller starring Jimmy Stewart, in which Ellington has a cameo role as a pianist named Pie Eye. This was followed by the sound track for *Paris Blues*, a drama in which Paul Newman and Sidney Poitier play American musicians living in Paris.

Ellington also worked on musical plays, with no success. An updated *Jump for Joy*, another musical set in South Africa,

Ellington gives trombone lessons to actor Paul Newman during the filming of Paris Blues. *This movie was the second feature film for which Ellington wrote the soundtrack.*

Irving Townsend, a record producer who worked with Ellington, said that Ellington took the making of records very seriously. In a 1960 magazine article, reprinted in Beyond Category, *Townsend writes:*

"Duke Ellington arrives at a record date with the same sense of timing he follows for every appearance, whether it be from the wings of a theatre, or out of a taxi, or out of a shower. . . . He has nurtured the reputation he has made for always being late, because it allows him the freedom to time his entrance to suit his sense of drama. . . . In our years of recording together, I've known Duke to arrive an hour early, two hours late, and at every point between these two extremes. I have never known him to arrive anywhere at the wrong time."

and a version of *The Blue Angel,* called *Pousse-Café,* were all failures. When *Pousse-Café*'s trouble-plagued production finally opened in 1966, one typical headline read, "Pousse-Café Called Dismal Disaster." It closed after only three performances. Ellington's failure over the years to mount a successful Broadway-style musical is something of a mystery. Perhaps it was that his music was too private, his sound too tied up with the individuals in his orchestra. Such music might not translate well to the larger, less personal scale of the theater.

Slimming Down

The late 1950s rejuvenated Ellington not only musically but personally. For virtually all of his adult life, Ellington had been overweight, even for his large frame. At one point, he tipped the scales at 260 pounds. Duke's love for eating was leg-endary; an entire chapter in his memoirs is devoted to favorite foods. According to one story he once ate thirty-two hot dogs at a sitting. A typical dinner might encompass two steaks, lobster with butter, a double order of fries, salad, a bowl of tomatoes, coffee, and a special "Ellington dessert" with three slices of cake, three kinds of ice cream, and three different toppings. Duke loved ice cream so much, in fact, that he carried a silver spoon with him at all times in case the urge struck.

In some ways Ellington was obsessed with his health; he constantly imagined the worst, always carried a doctor's bag filled with vitamin pills and protein tablets, and consulted Arthur Logan daily about his well-being. In general, though, Ellington abused his health. He had more or less given up drinking after seeing the effects of alcoholism on friends—"I retired undefeated champ," he once remarked. Still, he did drink in moderation. He also smoked a couple of packs of cigarettes a day, never exercised—he claimed his only exercise was walking downstairs from his apartment—and always closed hotel room windows to avoid what he called "fresh-air poisoning."

Now, after years of urging from Logan, Ellington finally agreed to lose weight. He invented a diet of steak, grapefruit, salad, and black coffee and lost thirty-five pounds in a year. He lost so much weight that on one occasion, while conducting a symphony orchestra in New Haven, Connecticut, his tuxedo pants started to fall down. Ellington had to hitch them up with one hand while conducting with the other, as portions of the orchestra were reduced to helpless laughter. When the piece was over, Ellington had to maneuver his pants into position before he could turn and take a bow. He wrote in his memoirs, "The musicians in the symphony continued to laugh long after I had left the stage. But my doctor was happy with the overall results!"[116]

Overseas Travel

Officially Ellington lived in New York, but as he often said, New York was just where he collected mail. His true home was on the road. He loved the privacy of hotel rooms, and he loved room service—as a black man, he was still sometimes insulted in restaurants, and he disliked being interrupted by fans during meals. Ellington stayed in touch with friends by telephone. Photographer Gordon Parks, a longtime friend, once remarked, "If a telephone rang within ten yards of him he went for it." Ellington himself called the telephone "the greatest invention since peanut brittle. . . . The only way to keep me from an-

swering one is to padlock my lips. Even then, I'll try sign language."[117]

Increasingly Ellington's travels involved overseas tours. These were often sponsored by the U.S. State Department as a means of promoting America abroad. In 1958 the band appeared in England for the first time in twenty-five years, where Duke was presented to Queen Elizabeth II. By all accounts the two royals—one a queen by birth, the other a duke by natural inclination—charmed each other thoroughly. Ellington told the queen how beautiful she looked. Later, when lyricist Don George commented on his skill at charming women, Ellington said, "It's very simple. You just tell the Queen of England the same thing you tell little Paula who works down at the pool hall."[118] Despite his joking manner, Ellington seemed genuinely delighted to have made Elizabeth's acquaintance. In her honor he later wrote a piece called *The Queen's Suite.* He recorded it, had a single copy pressed, and sent it to Buckingham Palace.

In addition to Europe, Ellington also traveled to Latin America, the Middle and Far East, the Caribbean, Africa, Australia, and the Soviet Union. Everywhere, Ellington received honors, including a meeting with the pope, a special Ellington edition of the Paris newspaper *Le Figaro* on his birthday, and an audience with another royal jazz fan, the king of Thailand. Comparing the king with a legendary jazz pianist, Ellington later commented, "His Majesty is the Art Tatum of monarchs."[119]

Travel affected the Ellington compositions to a degree. Although he and Strayhorn were fascinated by the unusual music they heard, they did not include

"It Should Be Admired but Not Analyzed"

These notes, reprinted in Mercer Ellington's Duke Ellington in Person, *were written by Duke Ellington after he met Queen Elizabeth II. The memories he mentions helped inspire his work* The Queen's Suite, *which was written in her honor.*

"1) *The Single Petal of a Rose.* So delicate, fragile, gentle, luminous. Only God could make one, and like love it should be admired but not analyzed.

2) *Mocking Bird in the Sunset.* While speeding across Florida from Tampa to West Palm Beach at 80 m.p.h. It was in the half-light of sunset that we passed a bird. It seemed to call to us. We would have liked to have gone back and thanked the bird, but we were much too far down the road and we didn't know what kind of bird it was anyway. But the first phrase is the melody we heard.

3) *Lightning Bugs and Frogs.* It was a hot summer night on the south shore of the Ohio River, a vast clearing with a backdrop of tall silhouetted trees, against which a million lightning bugs were weaving a spangled scrim [translucent backdrop], a design in symphonic splendor, while the frogs in the orchestra pit (pond in the foreground) provided the audio accompaniment.

4) *Northern Lights.* Up in Quebec. All night we watched this, the most majestic stage show I ever saw. It was like being a short man standing behind many tall people at Radio City Music Hall or the Palladium. You can't actually see the performers. You only see lights or shadows, or reflections of the actors' movements. The prima ballerina, the heavy, the thirty-six girl kickers, the quartette, are all there simultaneously, all night, only magnified a million times. And then when you stop, get out of the car, and look straight up overhead, it's all going on up there, too. This is terrifying.

5) *Le Sucrier Velours* [velvet sugar] is the name of a bird in France. I have seen pictures of it and I think it is a good name for the bird. But after thinking more, I believe a more fitting sight, that encroaches on the domain or sense of taste, is the almost-moustache, the fuzz over the corners of the upper lip of a sweet girl.

6) *Apes and Peacocks.* From the Bible: I Kings 10:22. For the King had at sea a navy of Tarshish with the navy of Hiram: once in three years came the navy of Tarshish bringing gold and silver, ivory, and apes and peacocks."

Ellington and band members are welcomed by dancers on the island of Ceylon in 1963. The orchestra's visit to Ceylon was part of a world tour sponsored by the U.S. State Department to promote America abroad.

specific elements, such as Indian raga forms or Japanese tonality, into their pieces. Instead they were inspired to write new pieces in their familiar style. Among these were "Impressions of the Far East" and "Ad Lib on Nippon." (The Japanese word for Japan is Nippon.) These two pieces were later reworked into the lengthy *Far East Suite.*

Throughout the 1960s and into the 1970s, Ellington received numerous honors and awards from all over the world. Although he professed to have little interest

in them, they are listed carefully in his memoirs, a compilation that takes up fifteen pages.

He received the keys to eighteen cities, awards from seven states, and honorary degrees from nearly twenty colleges and universities, including Columbia, Yale, Brown, and Howard. Ellington had already met several presidents, but now came official recognition for his contributions to American music. President Dwight D. Eisenhower gave him the President's Award for Special Merit. President

Lyndon B. Johnson gave him the President's Gold Medal and appointed him to the National Council of the Arts.

Honors from other countries also flowed in: the king of Ethiopia, Haile Selassie, awarded him the Emperor's Star, and French president Georges Pompidou gave him France's highest honor, the Legion of Honor. The African nations of Togo and Chad issued stamps in his honor. (The United States, which does not put living people on its stamps, issued an Ellington stamp in 1986). And in 1971 the Royal Swedish Academy of Music made him its first nonclassical member in its two-hundred-year history.

Ellington remained popular with fans and critics as well. Influential magazines such as *downbeat* and *Melody Maker* consistently placed him first in their polls. The recording industry regularly honored Ellington. He received, among other awards, eleven Grammys and the Lifetime Achievement Award from the National Academy of Recording Arts and Sciences. In all, over three hundred plaques, medals, and other honorary items awarded Ellington are now in the Smithsonian Institution. As John Edward Hasse wrote, "No American composer had ever been so widely honored, nationally and internationally, as Duke Ellington."[120]

"An Appalling Insult"

And yet Ellington was passed up for America's most prestigious musical honor, the Pulitzer Prize. In 1965 the three-person Pulitzer award jury unanimously recommended to its advisory board that Ellington receive a special prize for his forty

Ellington, donning a cap and gown, is awarded an honorary doctorate of music degree at Columbia University in 1973.

years of brilliant music. The recommendation was rejected, however, in a move widely regarded as racial. Two of the three jury members resigned, and the incident created international headlines. Musicians and composers around the world voiced their support of Ellington; the *San Francisco Chronicle* called the incident "an appalling insult."

Ellington's public reaction was typically wry. "Fate is being kind to me," he said. "Fate doesn't want me to be too famous too young." To a reporter, he said, "It doesn't matter. All I do is compose music. I can't afford to get bugged."[121] Privately, however, it must have been a slap in the face to a man who had long sought recognition as a serious American composer. As if to compensate, the City of New York later that year awarded him its Bronze Medal for "outstanding contributions to [New York's] life and the world of music." At the same time, *Esquire* magazine named him one of the "hundred best people in the world."

The Seventieth Birthday

Ellington was not a big fan of birthdays. He said they reminded him that he was getting older. His closest friends and colleagues had once conspired to surprise Ellington on his sixtieth birthday, but the plan backfired.

Ellington's writing habits had always been haphazard, and many of his pieces did not have clear sheet music. As a sixtieth birthday gift, Billy Strayhorn, Irving Townsend, Arthur Logan, and Mercer Ellington transcribed over thirty years' worth of music from recordings and notes into twenty-four leather-bound volumes. But Ellington's reaction was lukewarm. He was not interested in the past; he felt that having his music catalogued meant that his life was over, and he was not ready for that. Logan recalled, "He made polite noises and kissed us all, but, you know, the son of a bitch didn't even bother to take it home."[122] Their precious gift is now in the Smithsonian.

Despite this attitude, Ellington took pleasure in a party held for his seventieth birthday in 1969 at the White House. The guests included Ellington's friends and family, as well as such luminaries, or celebrities, as Dizzy Gillespie, Willie "the Lion" Smith, Benny Goodman, writers Stanley Dance and Leonard Feather, singers Mahalia Jackson, Cab Calloway, and Billy Eckstine, clergymen from several denominations, and assorted politicians and dignitaries. Everyone sang "Happy Birthday," accompanied by amateur pianist Richard Nixon, and an all-star band played a ninety-minute, all-Ellington con-

President Nixon presents Ellington with the Presidential Medal of Freedom during the bandleader's seventieth birthday party at the White House. The birthday gala was attended by friends and family of Ellington, as well as famous celebrities and politicians.

cert. President Nixon made a speech in which he said, "In the royalty of American music, no man swings more or stands higher than the Duke."[123]

The climax of the evening came when Nixon presented his guest of honor with the highest award the United States gives a civilian, the Presidential Medal of Freedom. Gazing out at a sea of well-wishers, Ellington remarked, "There is no place I would rather be tonight, except in my mother's arms." Ellington embraced Nixon and kissed him twice on each cheek. Nixon, who was generally uncomfortable with physical contact, recoiled slightly and asked, "Why four kisses?" Ellington just smiled and said, "One for each cheek." Soon after, the Nixons retired to bed. Vice President Spiro Agnew serenaded the assembled guests with Ellington pieces on the piano, and a jam session with dancing lasted until 2 A.M.

This event at the White House, where his father had once served as a butler, was perhaps the high point of all the many honors Ellington received. But Ellington was not a person who liked to rest on his laurels. The night after the presidential celebration, the band played a modest gig in Oklahoma City.

The First Sacred Concert

Ellington had always been a religious man. As a boy he had attended two church services every Sunday, and his parents had instilled in him a deep faith. After his mother died, he wore a crucifix around his neck every day, and as he grew older, he became increasingly interested in spiritual questions.

In 1965 Ellington was asked to write a piece in honor of the new Grace Cathedral in San Francisco. Ellington responded with the first of his three sacred concerts—the last major works he would write and the ones that he considered his most important. The sacred concerts let Ellington celebrate his personal beliefs aloud. As Ellington scholar Mark Tucker noted, "Up until this time Ellington's faith had been a private matter. With these late sacred works he found a public forum for expressing long-held personal beliefs."[124] Ellington thought of them like Handel's *Messiah*—as works that brought religion and entertainment together into a celebration for all people. He tried to put into them his feelings about humankind's essential equality. As he wrote in the notes for the first concert, "Every man prays in his own language, and there is no language that God does not understand."[125]

The concert premiered in the fall of 1965, an event that made headlines across the country. It featured the orchestra plus two choirs, three solo singers, and dancer Bunny Briggs, who performed during a section called "David Danced Before the Lord with All His Might." The music aroused strong passions. Some members of the clergy were shocked at the very idea of jazz in a church; others welcomed it as a bridge between religion and daily life. Some critics found the music and words simplistic, or overly simplified. One complained that the concert was "commonplace" and "embarrassing." On the other hand, critic Raymond Horricks called it a "remarkable . . . synthesis of Western Christianity [with] African roots and Pantheism [worship of all gods], gospel singing, the chronicles of the Bible, the aspirations of the New Testament and, not

The orchestra rehearses for their 1966 sacred concert performance at England's Coventry Cathedral.

least, the extra problems faced by mankind in our modern society."[126]

Much of the evening was taken up with reworked ideas from the past, such as the lovely, gospel-tinged "Come Sunday." However, several sections were new, and one of these—"In the Beginning, God"—won a Grammy for best original jazz composition. Public television also prepared two documentaries from the concert's rehearsals and performance; one of them, "Duke Ellington: Love You Madly," won an Emmy Award.

Over the next few years Ellington was asked to present the concert nearly fifty times, including performances at Coventry Cathedral in England and at Temple Emanu-el, a Jewish synagogue in Beverly Hills, California. Ellington said that the work was "successful beyond my wildest dreams."[127] It kept his creative juices flowing for several more years, until his career was slowed by the deaths of his closest collaborators and, finally, stopped by his own death.

10 The Final Years

Ideas? Oh, man. I got a million dreams. That's all I do is dream, all the time.

—Duke Ellington

All his life Ellington had gone to great lengths to keep his personal life and his public work separate. During the mid-1960s, however, Ellington's family and his extended family, the orchestra, became linked in one important way when his son Mercer rejoined the band. Since leaving the band some years before, Mercer had worked at a variety of jobs within the music business, including a successful stint as a New York City disk jockey. But in 1963 he rejoined the trumpet section. Soon he took over as the band's manager as well, after longtime road manager Al Celley's failing eyesight forced him to retire.

Mercer later described the job as a combination of "psychologist, mathematician, and private detective."[128] He was responsible for making sure that everyone in the band got on the right bus or plane, that hotel accommodations were in order, that unsatisfactory musicians were fired and new ones hired, and that a hundred other tasks got done every day. One thing that made the job especially difficult for him was that he was now in the position of bossing around people like Cootie

Williams, Johnny Hodges, and Harry Carney—men who had helped raise him from boyhood.

The job sometimes required forceful words and actions. For instance, there was

Ellington practices with his son Mercer, who rejoined the band in 1963 and took over as manager. Mercer found it difficult to relate to his often overbearing and self-absorbed father.

a superstitious belief among band members that those who first took their seats for a performance were in the greatest danger of losing their jobs; everyone was reluctant to take the stage, and the band was notorious for running late. Mercer recalled, "I started beefing [complaining], hollering, and screaming, and in some cases getting into fisticuffs [fistfights] in order to straighten this situation out."[129] The angry musicians would play poorly, and Duke would in turn blame his son.

Mercer and his father had a strange and often uncomfortable relationship. Ellington was a genius, and like many geniuses he was completely self-absorbed. As far as he was concerned, the world revolved around him. The opening line of the section devoted to his son in Duke's memoirs reveals a little about their relationship. It reads, "My son, Mercer Ellington, is dedicated to maintaining the luster of his father's image."[130]

Duke was fiercely protective of his family, but at the same time he could be extremely harsh toward them. After Billy Strayhorn began working with the band, for instance, Mercer's compositions for the band—which had showed considerable promise—were neglected. Mercer had to let other bands play them for free, just to get them heard in public at all.

When Mercer was younger and decided to start his own band, his father helped him enroll in the prestigious Juilliard music school—despite the older Ellington's contempt for formal education—and then, according to Mercer, sabotaged the younger Ellington's efforts to establish himself. Among other things, Mercer wrote, Duke stole good musicians away from his son and forced Mercer's record label to put out inferior versions.

"Pop never encouraged or discouraged me, but his every act was to keep my interest in another band from amounting to anything. He had made up his mind, out of superstition, that it was bad luck to have two bands in show business with the same name."[131]

Strayhorn and Hodges Pass On

By the late 1960s it seemed to Ellington that he was surrounded by illness and death. Billy Strayhorn, while helping prepare the First Sacred Concert in 1965, underwent the first of several operations for cancer of the esophagus. Soon he could no longer travel. He and Ellington spoke frequently by phone, however, and seemed almost telepathic in their collaborations. On one occasion, they began work on "In the Beginning, God" while separated by three thousand miles. Each wrote a rough idea based on phone conversations. When they compared manuscripts, they found that the two pieces began and ended with the same notes, and most of the main melodic ideas were identical.

By early 1967 Strayhorn weighed eighty pounds. He was hospitalized most of the time and could eat only liquified food through a straw. He continued to work from the hospital. Strayhorn's old friend Lena Horne visited and cared for him almost daily, nursing him at her home in California at one point. Strayhorn passed away, in Horne's arms, on May 31, 1967. He was fifty-one years old.

Ruth Ellington called her brother in Reno, Nevada, to break the news. Ellington cried, then sat down and wrote a tribute to his friend. It read, in part:

> Poor little Swee'Pea, Billy Strayhorn, William Thomas Strayhorn, the biggest human being who ever lived. . . . His greatest virtue, I think, was his honesty, not only to others but to himself. . . . His patience was incomparable and unlimited. He had no aspirations to enter into any kind of competition, yet the legacy he leaves, his *oeuvre* [work], will never be less than the ultimate on the highest plateau of culture. . . . God bless Billy Strayhorn.[132]

Ellington was more deeply affected by Strayhorn's death than by anything since the death of his mother. Otto Hardwick said, "Strayhorn's death was the one thing I know of that *really* touched Duke. The *one* thing."[133] Within three months the Ellington band was recording its heartfelt tribute album, . . . *And His Mother Called Him Bill*.

Others around Ellington also became ill. Drummer Sam Woodyard was in and out of the band due to bad health, Paul Gonsalves was having problems related to his epic alcohol and drug habits, and both Cootie Williams and Lawrence Brown were hospitalized for surgery. Then, in 1969, another major blow came. Johnny Hodges, the center of the Ellington sound, had a heart seizure and was forced to leave the band. The next year Hodges suffered a fatal heart attack. As he had done in the past, Ellington mourned the loss privately, and he publicly honored his colleague by retiring those pieces most associated with Hodges. "Johnny is not replaceable," Duke said flatly. "Because of this great loss our band will never sound the same."[134]

No Slowing Down

Ellington's own health problems were becoming severe. He had always been handsome, with limitless energy; in his prime, Ellington looked ten years younger than his age. Now, however, the heavy bags under his eyes, which he called "accumulations of virtue," became more pronounced. His movements slowed, his speech was even more careful than before, and he tired easily. He also became increasingly private. As Rex Stewart put it, "The hail fellow, well met, who was a buddy to his boys, [was] no longer there—and understandably so."[135]

As he entered his seventies, health problems and years of hard work had begun to take their toll on Ellington's once boundless energy and young-looking appearance.

Still, Ellington was determined to keep the band alive. The band made more tours, including successful return jaunts to the Soviet Union, Far East, South America, and Eastern Europe. Ellington also brought an eight-member version of the band to the Rainbow Room, a well-known nightclub in New York. Often he was accompanied on his tours by Fernanda de Castro Monte, a blonde singer nicknamed the Contessa who was twenty years younger than Ellington and who spoke five languages. She acted as a combination secretary-bodyguard to Ellington, making travel arrangements and keeping unwanted well-wishers or other visitors away.

Ellington also wrote his memoirs. *Music Is My Mistress* was handwritten over the course of several years on whatever scraps of hotel stationery were handy, then transcribed by Ellington's friend Stanley Dance. The result is a version of Ellington's life that downplays the negative. Its publisher, Doubleday, nearly created a disaster when it printed thousands of copies with a brown cover, not knowing that Ellington had a superstition about the color brown. He refused to distribute the book until—at great trouble and expense—it was redone in blue.

Among Ellington's new compositions was a ballet, *The River*, commissioned by the American Ballet Theatre and premiered in 1970 at Lincoln Center with choreography by Alvin Ailey. He also wrote "Afro-Eurasian Eclipse," which premiered at the 1970 Monterey Jazz Festival. And he worked on an hour-long comic opera called *Queenie Pie*, commissioned by public television station WNET but never completed.

Foremost in his mind, however, were two new sacred concerts. The second, an evening's worth of new material, pre-

Conserving His Energy

As Ellington grew older, his son recalls in Duke Ellington in Person, *he became more conscious of preserving what remained of his failing health.*

"He was very resourceful in the way he conserved his energy. He studied his diet and geared his physical disposition to do the job he had to do. That is why some said he was a hypochondriac. . . . Pop learned to control his mind as well as his body. He knew that as he grew older he could easily develop high blood pressure, so sometimes, when he seemed to be furious, he would suddenly stop in the middle of a conversation or argument and go off and read or watch television to relax himself. He did this because he realized what he was doing was unhealthy for him, not out of consideration for the person he was screaming at."

Ellington's orchestra during a 1972 Second Sacred Concert performance at St. Paul's Cathedral in Toronto. The concert featured new material and received mostly positive reviews.

miered at the Cathedral of Saint John the Divine in New York in 1968 before an audience of six thousand. It required the full orchestra plus several solo singers and a hundred-voice choir. The concert was later performed in Connecticut, Minnesota, France, Sweden, Spain, and elsewhere. The reviews were mixed but generally positive; *downbeat* magazine, which rates performances with a star system, gave the concert's recorded version "all the stars in God's heaven."

Much of Ellington's energy in his last years was spent on the Third Sacred Concert, which premiered at Westminster Abbey in London in 1973. It is quieter, more serene, and more introspective than the other sacred concerts. Many of Ellington's best players were gone by this point, and there was little rehearsal time. Ellington wisely chose to focus on a few soloists—Harry Carney, himself, and singer Alice Babs. Critic Gary Giddins wrote of the evening, "It is illuminating, not least for showing how Ellington coped with the insoluble problem of having outlived his band."[136]

Ellington was so weak by the Westminster Abbey performance that he had to leave the stage when there was no piano part. During the European tour that had preceded the performance, Mercer had noticed his father's exhaustion; after only a few hours of rehearsal, this once vibrant man had to rest. "Flying the Atlantic at his age and going into rehearsal without much sleep required strength, but he knew that he always did his best work under pressure," Mercer wrote, adding that even Ellington himself had to admit that the pace had slackened. "I think for the first time in his life he knew he wasn't capable of it."[137]

The Tempo Slows

The fall of 1973 brought more personal tragedy. In September Ben Webster, the star of so many glorious Ellington recordings, died. In November Ellington's friend and physician, Arthur Logan, also died. He had been standing on a bridge, inspecting

Ellington was diagnosed with lung cancer in 1963, but refused to slow down. This photo was taken after he received the French Legion of Honor in 1973, less than a year before his death.

a site for a new hospital, when he fell. There is speculation that he was thrown by two men who had mugged him.

Ellington, who was overseas at the time, was distraught by Logan's death; it affected him perhaps even more than Strayhorn's. Marian Logan, the doctor's widow, recalled that Ellington's first response when she told him the news was to ask, "What am I going to do without my doctor?"[138] Soon Ellington was convinced that he would not last another six months himself. Mercer Ellington wrote, "He felt there was no one left in the world to take care of him. What would happen to him? It was as though he were alone in the wilderness."[139]

Logan was one of only two people— the other was Ruth—who knew how ill Duke really was. In 1963 Cootie Williams had been diagnosed with lung problems while the band was in Houston. The medical center there had suggested that the whole band be checked, and several members of the band showed severe problems. Six months later Ellington, a lifelong smoker, was diagnosed with lung cancer. For many years Ellington was able to keep it a secret and to somehow keep going. He even tried self-invented devices to delay the cancer, including shots of vitamin B12 and a process in which he soaked cigarettes in menthol before smoking them.

Finally, in March 1974, Ellington had to leave the band in midtour and check into New York's Columbia Presbyterian Hospital. He had a piano by his bed, and he continued to work—on *Queenie Pie*, on a ballet suite called *The Three Black Kings*, and on plans for recording the Third Sacred Concert. His eyesight was fading, but he continued to talk into a cassette recorder. Toward the end Ellington also developed severe pneumonia. Still, right up until the last moment Ellington kept his wit alive: at one point, he told his old friend Sonny Greer to be sure to take care of their female friends—their "nieces"— up in Harlem.

The Finale

On Ellington's seventy-fifth birthday, the orchestra performed selections from the Third Sacred Concert at New York's Central Presbyterian Church, but Ellington was too ill to attend. In May, when two longtime band members died—trombonist Tyree Glenn and saxophonist Paul Gonsalves—no one had the heart to tell Ellington. Then, on May 24, 1974, at 3:10 A.M., with his son Mercer there, Duke Ellington died. His death came as he had predicted—almost exactly six months after the death of Arthur Logan.

For a short time the bodies of Glenn, Gonsalves, and Ellington were laid out together for public viewing in the same mortuary. The public's demand to view the beloved bandleader was overwhelming—a total of sixty-five thousand people came, and the funeral parlor stayed open twenty-four hours a day. People shook his hand, kissed him, and left mementos in his coffin.

Condolence calls and telegrams poured in by the thousands. Richard Nixon said, "The wit, taste, intelligence and elegance that Duke Ellington brought to his music have made him, in the eyes of millions of people both here and abroad, America's foremost composer." Singer

"A Citizen of the World"

This passage from Mark Tucker's Duke Ellington Reader *is an excerpt from the eulogy that Ellington's longtime friend Stanley Dance delivered at his funeral.*

"In the truest sense of the phrase, he was a citizen of the world. That is a cliché perhaps, but how few are those who *deserve* it as he did. He was loved throughout the whole world, at all levels of society. . . .

Song titles say a good deal. 'Mood Indigo,' 'Sophisticated Lady,' 'Caravan,' 'Solitude,' 'Don't Get Around Much Anymore,' 'I'm Beginning to See the Light' and 'Satin Doll' are part of the fabric of Twentieth-century life. But the popular song hits are only a small part of Duke Ellington's priceless legacy to mankind. . . .

Duke Ellington knew that what some called genius was really the exercise of gifts which stemmed from God . . . [and] Duke knew the good news was Love, of God and his fellow men. He proclaimed the message in his sacred concerts, grateful for an opportunity to acknowledge something of which he stood in awe, a power he considered above his human limitations. He firmly believed what the mother he worshipped also believed, that he had been blessed at birth. He reached out to people with his music and drew them to himself. . . .

It is Memorial Day [today], when those who died for the free world are properly remembered. Duke Ellington never lost faith in his country, and he served it well. His music will go on serving it for years to come."

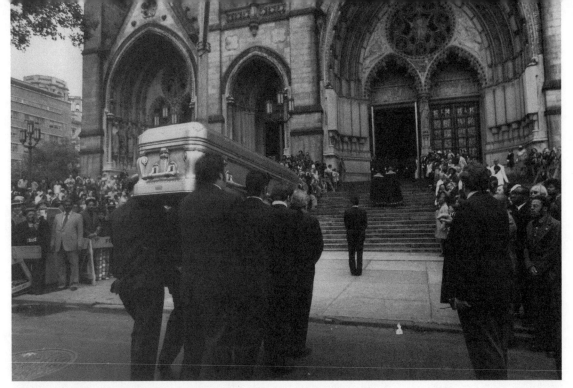

Thousands of fans turned out to pay tribute to Ellington during funeral services at the Cathedral of Saint John the Divine.

Dinah Shore said, "When someone like Duke Ellington dies, we haven't lost him. Every time I sing one of his songs, I realize how lucky I am and how lucky we all are to have his exquisite talent to draw joy and sustenance from." Longtime friend Ella Fitzgerald perhaps summed it up best with her simple words: "It's a very sad day. A genius has passed."[140]

Funeral services were held for Ellington at Saint John the Divine on Memorial Day, and he was buried that same day next to his parents in Woodlawn Cemetery. At the service ten thousand people packed the cathedral, with another twenty-five hundred standing outside listening to loudspeakers. Mercer recalled arriving at the cathedral and being astonished at the huge crowds milling in the street: "'The people haven't gone in yet,' someone said.

'I think they are the ones who can't get in,' I replied."[141]

Ellington's friend Stanley Dance delivered the eulogy. Among the musicians performing were pianists Earl "Fatha" Hines and Mary Lou Williams. Ella Fitzgerald sang "In My Solitude" and "Just a Closer Walk with Thee." But it was a recording of Johnny Hodges and Alice Babs from the Second Sacred Concert, echoing through the church as the congregation filed out, that was perhaps the most moving of all the tributes. Mercer Ellington also recalled the huge crowds that waited to say goodbye to their friend and hero as the funeral procession drove slowly away through the streets of Harlem. "It was a matter of belonging," Mercer wrote. "Hadn't he always referred to *my people?*"[142]

We Loved Him Madly

I think all the musicians in jazz should get together on one certain day and get down on their knees to thank Duke.

—Miles Davis

Before his death Ellington had promised that the band would play a concert in Bermuda, with or without him. As it happened, the date fell just after Ellington's funeral. In his memoirs, Mercer wrote, "I knew what the Old Man would have done under the circumstances, and I had no inhibitions about doing it. So I almost simultaneously rehearsed the orchestra and made arrangements for the funeral."[143] Immediately after the ceremonies, the band flew to Bermuda; Mercer told a reporter: "The Duke would have wanted it that way."[144]

Many Ellington friends and colleagues soon followed him in death. Four months later Harry Carney, the rock-solid bottom of the Ellington sound for so many years, passed away. Evie Ellis died in 1976 and was buried alongside Ellington. Ray Nance followed in 1976, Freddie Jenkins in 1978, Barney Bigard in 1980, and Russell Procope and Cat Anderson in 1981. Sonny Greer died in 1982, Juan Tizol in 1984, Cootie Williams in 1985, and Lawrence Brown and Sam Woodyard in 1988.

To this day Mercer Ellington continues the difficult, brave task of maintaining his father's legacy. He leads the orchestra in performing around the world. He donated hundreds of hours of private Ellington tapes to Danish Radio (Mercer's wife is Danish). He completed his father's unfinished opera *Queenie Pie*. And he recently donated Ellington's papers, scores, and other memorabilia to the Smithsonian—a treasure trove that will keep scholars busy for decades. Ellington, who never had time to become respectably institutionalized in life, will at last be honored with complete scores that will let repertory groups and college bands play his music properly for the first time.

Most of Ellington's recordings have been reissued on compact disc; one of the best is *The Blanton-Webster Band*, a compilation of the glorious early-1940s recordings. Seven years after his death one of Ellington's fondest goals—a hit Broadway musical—was finally achieved when *Sophisticated Ladies*, based on his music, became a smash success. In 1987 Lincoln Center began an annual series of Ellington concerts. Pianist and singer Bobby Short is trying to raise money for a statue of Ellington in Central Park, though reportedly he has run into problems with the proposed design: Ellington and his piano, held aloft

Mercer still leads the Ellington orchestra, and is dedicated to the preservation of his famous father's legacy for future generations of music lovers.

by nine nude women. And in 1991 Congress established the Smithsonian Jazz Masterworks Orchestra, whose work will include regular concerts and broadcasts of Ellington music. As John Edward Hasse put it, "In the 1990s, two decades after his death, Ellington seemed to be much larger than life [and] seemed to be commanding his biggest comeback yet."[145]

The music departments of most universities and colleges have been slow to teach his music, partly because their re-

---

"A Sense of Possibility"

In this passage reprinted in Mark Tucker's Duke Ellington Reader, *critic Martin Williams catalogues the staggering amount of music Ellington produced during his lifetime:*

"Ellington left an enormous body of music: simple songwriting; theater songs; background music for dramatic films and television melodrama; solo piano works; duets for piano and bass; music for small jazz ensembles from sextet through octet; hundreds of short instrumental compositions for jazz orchestra; extended works, usually suites, for large jazz ensemble, sometimes with singers and (for the later 'sacred' concerts) also with tap dancers; works for jazz ensemble and symphony orchestra combined. . . . Ellington is probably the largest and most challenging subject in American music for our scholars, our critics, our musicologists, our music historians."

Ellington posthumously achieved his goal of a hit Broadway musical with
Sophisticated Ladies. *The hugely successful musical, which premiered in*
1981, was based on Ellington's music.

liance on written scores conflicts with Ellington's reluctance to write things down. Still, Ellington's music remains vibrantly alive. Musicians and composers worldwide study him intently, and he has directly influenced such important performers as Charles Mingus, Carla Bley, David Murray, Lester Bowie, and Wynton Marsalis.

Every day—perhaps every minute of every day—someone, somewhere, is playing or humming or singing or listening to one of Ellington's immortal melodies. If that person changes the music slightly to reflect a personal taste or vision, Ellington would surely approve; his music contains a spirit that loves a continual state of change. Ellington did not even like to write endings. As Clark Terry once said, Duke always wanted to make his music sound as if it were still *going* somewhere, even when it had ended.

Notes

Introduction: "We Love You Madly"

1. Quoted in John Edward Hasse, *Beyond Category: The Life and Genius of Duke Ellington.* New York: Simon and Schuster, 1993, p. 404.

Chapter 1: The Early Years

2. Quoted in Hasse, *Beyond Category*, p. 32.
3. Mark Tucker, *Ellington: The Early Years.* Urbana and Chicago: University of Illinois Press, 1991, p. 15.
4. Duke Ellington, *Music Is My Mistress.* New York: Doubleday, 1973, p. 10.
5. Ellington, *Music Is My Mistress*, p. x.
6. James Lincoln Collier, *Duke Ellington.* New York: Oxford University Press, 1987, p. 8.
7. Quoted in Hasse, *Beyond Category*, p. 23.
8. Ellington, *Music Is My Mistress*, p. 17.
9. Ellington, *Music Is My Mistress*, p. 27.
10. Richard O. Boyer, "The Hot Bach," *The New Yorker*, June 24, 1944. Reprinted in Mark Tucker, *The Duke Ellington Reader.* New York: Oxford University Press, 1993, p. 237.

Chapter 2: First Hints of Music

11. Collier, *Duke Ellington*, pp. 14–15.
12. Quoted in Hasse, *Beyond Category*, pp. 38–39.
13. Quoted in Hasse, *Beyond Category*, pp. 40–41.
14. Quoted in Hasse, *Beyond Category*, p. 36.
15. Ellington, *Music Is My Mistress*, p. 379.
16. Quoted in Hasse, *Beyond Category*, p. 38.
17. Hasse, *Beyond Category*, p. 38.
18. Quoted in Hasse, *Beyond Category*, p. 51.
19. Quoted in Hasse, *Beyond Category*, p. 51.
20. Ellington, *Music Is My Mistress*, p. 20.
21. Quoted in Hasse, *Beyond Category*, pp. 44–45.

22. Quoted in Hasse, *Beyond Category*, p. 45.
23. Quoted in Hasse, *Beyond Category*, pp. 53–54.
24. Quoted in Hasse, *Beyond Category*, p. 49.
25. Quoted in Hasse, *Beyond Category*, p. 49.

Chapter 3: Early Gigs

26. Quoted in Stanley Dance, *The World of Duke Ellington.* New York: Charles Scribner's Sons, 1970, p. 63.
27. Quoted in Hasse, *Beyond Category*, p. 58.
28. Quoted in Hasse, *Beyond Category*, p. 62.
29. Quoted in Tucker, *The Duke Ellington Reader*, p. 226.
30. Quoted in Hasse, *Beyond Category*, p. 70.
31. Quoted in Hasse, *Beyond Category*, p. 71.
32. Quoted in Hasse, *Beyond Category*, p. 75.
33. Quoted in Hasse, *Beyond Category*, p. 72.
34. Quoted in Collier, *Duke Ellington*, p. 296.
35. Quoted in Collier, *Duke Ellington*, p. 296.
36. Quoted in Hasse, *Beyond Category*, p. 345.
37. Collier, *Duke Ellington*, p. 253.
38. Quoted in Hasse, *Beyond Category*, pp. 80–81.
39. Quoted in Hasse, *Beyond Category*, p. 75.

Chapter 4: Breakthroughs

40. Ellington, *Music Is My Mistress*, p. 70.
41. Quoted in Peter Gammond, ed., *Duke Ellington: His Life and Music.* London: Phoenix House, 1958, p. 80.
42. Quoted in Tucker, *Ellington: The Early Years*, p. 23.
43. Quoted in Hasse, *Beyond Category*, p. 88.
44. Hasse, *Beyond Category*, pp. 92–93.
45. Quoted in Hasse, *Beyond Category*, p. 92.
46. Quoted in Hasse, *Beyond Category*, p. 78.
47. Quoted in Hasse, *Beyond Category*, p. 78.

48. Whitney Balliett, "Celebrating the Duke," *The New Yorker*, November 29, 1993, p. 136.

49. Balliett, "Celebrating the Duke," p. 136.

50. Quoted in Tucker, *The Duke Ellington Reader*, p. 228.

51. Barney Bigard, *With Louis and the Duke*. New York: Oxford University Press, 1986, pp. 45–46.

52. Mercer Ellington with Stanley Dance, *Duke Ellington in Person: An Intimate Memoir*. Boston: Houghton Mifflin, 1978, pp. 65–66.

53. Quoted in Dance, *The World of Duke Ellington*, p. 60.

54. Collier, *Duke Ellington*, p. 91.

55. Hasse, *Beyond Category*, p. 90.

56. Quoted in Dance, *The World of Duke Ellington*, p. 69.

57. Collier, *Duke Ellington*, p. 66.

58. Bigard, *With Louis and the Duke*, p. 49.

Chapter 5: The Heart of Harlem

59. Quoted in Hasse, *Beyond Category*, pp. 104–105.

60. Hasse, *Beyond Category*, p. 112.

61. Quoted in Hasse, *Beyond Category*, p. 150.

62. Rex Stewart, *Boy Meets Horn*. Ann Arbor: University of Michigan Press, 1991, p. 177.

63. Quoted in Hasse, *Beyond Category*, p. 147.

64. Quoted in Tucker, *The Duke Ellington Reader*, p. 113.

65. Quoted in Hasse, *Beyond Category*, p. 255.

66. Ellington, *Music Is My Mistress*, p. 471.

67. Quoted in Hasse, *Beyond Category*, p. 131.

68. Collier, *Duke Ellington*, p. 103.

Chapter 6: Fame and Change

69. Quoted in Hasse, *Beyond Category*, p. 179.

70. Quoted in Dance, *The World of Duke Ellington*, p. 11.

71. Quoted in Hasse, *Beyond Category*, p. 177.

72. Quoted in Hasse, *Beyond Category*, p. 170.

73. Quoted in Dance, *The World of Duke Ellington*, pp. 77–78.

74. Quoted in Collier, *Duke Ellington*, p. 157.

75. Quoted in Tucker, *The Duke Ellington Reader*, p. 244.

76. Quoted in Barry Ulanov, *Duke Ellington*. New York: Da Capo, 1946 and 1975, p. 151.

77. Bigard, *With Louis and the Duke*, p. 65.

78. Quoted in Hasse, *Beyond Category*, p. 210.

79. Hasse, *Beyond Category*, p. 195.

80. Quoted in Hasse, *Beyond Category*, p. 203.

81. Quoted in Hasse, *Beyond Category*, pp. 219–220.

82. Quoted in Collier, *Duke Ellington*, p. 195.

83. Quoted in Hasse, *Beyond Category*, p. 221.

84. Stewart, *Boy Meets Horn*, p. 182.

85. Quoted in Hasse, *Beyond Category*, p. 224.

86. Quoted in Ulanov, *Duke Ellington*, p. 217.

Chapter 7: The War Years

87. Quoted in Tucker, *The Duke Ellington Reader*, p. 269.

88. Quoted in Hasse, *Beyond Category*, p. 233.

89. Quoted in Hasse, *Beyond Category*, p. 215.

90. Quoted in Hasse, *Beyond Category*, p. 234.

91. Collier, *Duke Ellington*, p. 240.

92. Quoted in Dance, *The World of Duke Ellington*, p. 108.

93. Quoted in Hasse, *Beyond Category*, p. 241.

94. Quoted in Hasse, *Beyond Category*, p. 241.

95. "Reminiscing in Tempo," documentary, in *The American Experience*, PBS, 1990.

96. Quoted in Hasse, *Beyond Category*, p. 242.

97. Quoted in Hasse, *Beyond Category*, p. 248.

98. Quoted in Tucker, *The Duke Ellington Reader*, p. 266.

99. Quoted in Hasse, *Beyond Category*, p. 264.

100. Quoted in Hasse, *Beyond Category*, p. 279.

Chapter 8: Hard Times

101. Quoted in Collier, *Duke Ellington*, p. 255.

102. Quoted in Tucker, *The Duke Ellington Reader*, p. 121.

103. Quoted in Hasse, *Beyond Category,* p. 218.

104. Quoted in Hasse, *Beyond Category,* p. 256.

105. Quoted in Hasse, *Beyond Category,* p. 148.

106. Quoted in Don George, *Sweet Man: The Real Duke Ellington.* New York: G. P. Putnam's, 1981, p. 202.

107. Ellington, *Duke Ellington in Person*, p. 203.

108. Hasse, *Beyond Category*, p. 298.

109. Quoted in Hasse, *Beyond Category*, pp. 304–305.

110. Quoted in Hasse, *Beyond Category*, p. 305.

111. Quoted in Hasse, *Beyond Category*, p. 310.

112. Quoted in Hasse, *Beyond Category*, p. 321.

113. Balliett, "Celebrating the Duke."

Chapter 9: Honors at Home and Abroad

114. Quoted in Hasse, *Beyond Category*, p. 318.

115. Quoted in Tucker, *The Duke Ellington Reader*, p. 367.

116. Ellington, *Music Is My Mistress*, p. 390.

117. Quoted in Hasse, *Beyond Category*, p. 379.

118. Quoted in Don George, *Sweet Man*, p. 131.

119. Ellington, *Music Is My Mistress*, p. 384.

120. Hasse, *Beyond Category*, p. 377.

121. Quoted in Hasse, *Beyond Category*, p. 356.

122. Quoted in Hasse, *Beyond Category*, p. 336.

123. Quoted in Hasse, *Beyond Category*, p. 373.

124. Tucker, *The Duke Ellington Reader*, p. 317.

125. Quoted in Hasse, *Beyond Category*, p. 357.

126. Quoted in Hasse, *Beyond Category*, p. 358.

127. Quoted in Hasse, *Beyond Category*, p. 359.

Chapter 10: The Final Years

128. Quoted in Hasse, *Beyond Category*, p. 355.

129. Ellington, *Duke Ellington in Person*, p. 137.

130. Ellington, *Music Is My Mistress*, p. 41.

131. Ellington, *Duke Ellington in Person*, p. 90.

132. Quoted in Hasse, *Beyond Category*, p. 372.

133. Quoted in Dance, *The World of Duke Ellington*, p. 61.

134. Quoted in Hasse, *Beyond Category*, p. 380.

135. Stewart, *Boy Meets Horn*, p. 89.

136. Quoted in Hasse, *Beyond Category*, p. 384.

137. Ellington, *Duke Ellington in Person*, p. 193.

138. "Reminiscing in Tempo."

139. Ellington, *Duke Ellington in Person*, p. 198.

140. Quoted in Hasse, *Beyond Category*, p. 385.

141. Ellington, *Duke Ellington in Person*, p. 219.

142. Ellington, *Duke Ellington in Person*, p. 220.

Epilogue: We Loved Him Madly

143. Ellington, *Duke Ellington in Person*, pp. 215.

144. Quoted in Hasse, *Beyond Category*, p. 392.

145. Hasse, *Beyond Category*, p. 396.

For Further Reading

Stanley Dance, *The World of Duke Ellington*. New York: Charles Scribner's Sons, 1970. An excellent collection of interviews with Ellington and his colleagues, by a British-born writer who was also a close friend and collaborator of Ellington's.

Duke Ellington, *Music Is My Mistress*. New York: Doubleday, 1973. An interesting mixture of memoir, poetry, short essays, and travelogue by Ellington himself. It is relentlessly sunny and often shallow, but a valuable document nonetheless.

Mercer Ellington with Stanley Dance, *Duke Ellington in Person: An Intimate Memoir*. Boston: Houghton Mifflin, 1978. An entertaining, highly personal, and detailed memoir by Ellington's only child, cowritten with one of the maestro's closest friends and collaborators.

John Edward Hasse, *Beyond Category: The Life and Genius of Duke Ellington*. New York: Simon and Schuster, 1993. The definitive Ellington biography, far and away the best of the bunch; exhaustively researched, generous in spirit, and clearly written by a scholar of American music at the Smithsonian.

Additional Works Consulted

Whitney Balliett, "Celebrating the Duke," *The New Yorker*, November 29, 1993. A retrospective look at Ellington's music by *The New Yorker*'s longtime jazz critic.

Barney Bigard, *With Louis and the Duke*. New York: Oxford University Press, 1986. A memoir by a New Orleans–born clarinetist who spent many years with Ellington. Unpretentiously told in Bigard's own words.

Cab Calloway with Bryant Rollins, *Of Minnie the Moocher and Me*. New York: Thomas Crowell, 1976. An entertaining memoir by the great bandleader and vocalist, one of Ellington's rivals for popularity in their heyday.

James Lincoln Collier, *Duke Ellington*. New York: Oxford University Press, 1987. Good overviews of Ellington's world and recordings, though the style is dry and the attitude strangely contemptuous.

Robert Drew, director-producer, *On the Road with Duke Ellington*, Los Angeles, Direct Cinema, 1967. A video that follows Ellington on tour in the mid-1960s.

Peter Gammond, ed., *Duke Ellington: His Life and Music*. London: Phoenix House, 1958. A collection of essays, primarily by British writers, on various aspects of Ellington's career.

Don George, *Sweet Man: The Real Duke Ellington*. New York: G. P. Putnam's, 1981. A shamelessly self-serving backstage memoir by a lyricist who sometimes worked with Ellington. Plenty of racy stories about Ellington's success as a ladies' man.

Gene Lees, "The Enigma: Duke Ellington," in *Meet Me at Jim and Andy's: Jazz Musicians and Their World*. New York: Oxford University Press, 1988. A perceptive essay by a respected jazz writer.

Ken Rathenbury, *Duke Ellington: Jazz Composer*. New Haven: Yale University Press, 1990. Mostly technical, concentrating on close analyses of Ellington works, by a British musician and composer.

Rex Stewart, *Boy Meets Horn*. Ann Arbor: University of Michigan Press, 1991. A good memoir by one of Ellington's longtime musicians, trumpeter Stewart.

———, *Jazz Masters of the Thirties*. New York: Macmillan, 1972. A book about some of the greatest names in jazz by one of Ellington's longtime musicians.

Mark Tucker, "Duke Ellington, 1940–42." Liner notes to the three-CD collection *Duke Ellington: The Blanton-Webster Band*, RCA/Bluebird, 1986.

———, *Ellington: The Early Years*. Urbana and Chicago: University of Illinois Press, 1991. A detailed, scholarly volume on the period of Ellington's life before his rise to fame at the Cotton Club.

Mark Tucker, ed., *The Duke Ellington Reader*. New York: Oxford University Press, 1993. A valuable collection of writings by and about Ellington, from the earliest reviews of the Washingtonians to scholarly musical analyses of Ellington classics. A highlight is the famous 1944 *New Yorker* magazine profile, "The Hot Bach."

Barry Ulanov, *Duke Ellington*. New York: Da Capo, 1946 and 1975. An early biography by a professor and music scholar. The 1975 edition has not been updated and suffers from a lack of the information that came later in Ellington's life but has excellent interview material from people who knew and worked with him early on.

Index

Picture Credits

About the Author

Adam Woog, a former jazz critic for the *Seattle Times*, is the author of several books for young people and adults. Among his books for Lucent are *The United Nations*, *Poltergeists*, *The Importance of Harry Houdini*, and *The Importance of Louis Armstrong*. He lives with his wife and daughter in Seattle, Washington, not far from the mountains that inspired Duke Ellington's "Warm Valley."